DIRTY DARE

A MM SLAYERS HOCKEY NOVELLA

SLAYERS HOCKEY

MIRA LYN KELLY

Cover Designer: Najla Qamber, Najla Qamber Designs

Editor: Jennifer Miller

Proofreader: Kara Hildabrand

Proofreader: Katie Dunneback

1

Trevor
Off-Season

"Say it with me, little brother," Tammy sings through the car speaker. "No more jocks."

"No more jocks," I groan, turning left onto Old Wildren Road. Never again. And yeah, maybe I have a type, but whatever. I'll get over it.

The wooded country road twists and turns through another mile before splitting at the hand-painted sign for Little Lake Lane.

"Jesus, what am I doing back here?" My mom, sister, and I moved out of Wildren the summer after I graduated high school and started playing hockey for the Orators, Chicago's farm team down in Springfield. I loved it here, but after what happened when I left?

Maybe this was a mistake.

Tammy ignores the rhetorical part of the question and huffs.

"Getting out of Dodge so you don't have to spend the summer living in the same apartment with your cheating, asshole ex." She takes a bite of something crunchy, probably racing to get some food in her before the baby wakes up. "Retreating to a place where your life was simpler. I mean mostly. You know, except for *that*."

Right. That. Cameron Dorsey. The first jock.

First a lot of things.

"We're not talking about *that*." Ever.

She hums. "You sure *that* isn't part of why you chose Wildren?"

Why I always crack and end up spilling my damn feelings to my sister, I have no idea.

"Positive." It's ancient history, and if I had to guess, *that* is probably going to avoid me like the plague. *That* is probably married to a nice woman and has a nice life working in his nice family business just like he was always supposed to.

"Yeah, fuck *that*."

I grin. Okay, now I remember why. Two years older, Tammy's always had my back. And it's not like I've got anyone else to talk to about this stuff. No one else knows I'm a bi professional hockey player who, until a few months back, was in a relationship and living with a teammate for the better part of a year. A teammate whose professional jealousy and private insecurities drove him to betray me in a brutal way.

More crunching sounds through the car speaker, and then I hear Dominic's tiny squawk as he wakes up from his nap. The crunching gets faster. Tammy gulps. "Anyone know you're back?"

"Not before today." I'd been planning to lay low. Hide out in the cabin on the lake and decompress after the roller coaster season I've had.

Figured when I ducked into the Sew Shoppe to pick up the keys my old athletic director left me, no one would remember the kid who only lived here a few years. But that's not how small towns work. "Cora Michaels was working. She says hi. Also, Danny Nobbs just bought his first house. Party tonight. Found out your ex, Tino, got Crystal Miller *and* Nora Jacobs pregnant three weeks apart—"

"Douche!"

I laugh. "Right? And I'm invited to dinner at my old English teacher's place next week."

"Not bad for a just-rolling-into-town, Trev."

"Guess not."

Another protesting squawk sounds, and I can practically see my nephew's little hands flailing and his chubby face screwing up like he's going to rain down holy hell if he doesn't get my sister's full attention soon. Damn, I'm going to miss them.

For maybe the thousandth time today, I question my life choices.

Tammy makes one of those half-laugh, half-sigh noises, and I know that's a wrap. "I've got to go, little brother. Good luck getting all that peace and quiet you were after up there. And good luck with... *that* other thing too."

Not going to be an issue. "Love you, Sis. Give the squirt a cuddle for me."

I end the call and let myself *feel* being back here. Four years since I drove this secluded road, and my heart's pounding like I'm eighteen again, heading to the party of the year. Only as my pickup rolls down the quarter mile of crushed gravel drive in dire need of grading, I know the place I'm heading isn't the same.

Last time I was here, we'd just graduated, and Finch, the athletic director at the time, was having his annual end-of-year bash.

All the varsity players from all the sports throughout the year were invited to his cabin for a barbecue dinner, swimming, and a bonfire at his beach. It was tradition, but with each subsequent year, he got more hands-off. My year... and as it turned out, his last in the role of athletic director, the man handed me the keys to his place about six p.m. and headed back to his house in town, leaving the cabin in the hands of the kids he knew would take care of it the way he'd taken care of us.

That night, everything changed. All it took was one dare, a joke that the two captains kiss, and this low, simmering thing in my belly turned to a boil. Cam blew it off like the pro he was. Didn't bat an eye. Didn't bother with more than a snort before taking off to use the head. But me?

Not cool. Because in a wink, I could see that dare in action. Me kissing Cam. The guy I was always drawn to in a way that was different than with my other friends and who more than once left me wondering if I wanted to get closer or push him away.

I could see it. And I liked the look of it so damn much that I had to make some bullshit excuse about getting a swim in to cool off before anyone noticed the way my body was responding.

I dove straight into the lake and swam my ass out to the far side of the floating dock, where I hung off the back side, shaking. Asking myself what the hell was happening inside my head.

Within a minute, I heard the *lap, lap, lap* of someone swimming out. And then he was there, powerful legs treading in place. The defined muscles of his arms and shoulders even broader than mine bunching and flexing as he slicked his hair back from those serious, soulful eyes.

And, *yeah.*

Sigh.

Now, I'm the only one here. From the looks of it, maybe I'm the only one who's been here since Finch broke his hip down in Florida two years back and decided to stay. The property's overgrown. The cabin's in need of repairs. And maybe it's exactly what I need.

Maybe seeing this place looking nothing like the way I remember it is just the thing to get my head on straight before next season starts.

Cam

I'M RUNNING a sales report at the counter when the antique bell above the door sounds, signaling a customer. Or in this case, not a customer but my buddy Neil Watson. "Yo, Cam. You coming to Danny's tonight?"

I hate being the one who always says no to a party, but between work and water polo, more often than not, that's the way of it.

"Got practice, man. Say hi to everyone."

For anyone else, that would be the end of it. But Neil's that lifelong friend whose default setting is *all drama, all the time*. Sure enough, his head drops, and he heaves an exaggerated breath before taking an exaggerated step completely into the store.

It's close to closing, so we're empty, and I've got time. But even if we weren't, it wouldn't stop him.

I close the laptop and round the counter to meet him by the fishing equipment where he will accidentally, on purpose mix a couple reels of twenty-pound line in with the thirty.

"Hey, how'd it go with Judy last night?" He's been

trying to date this girl since the third grade, but she's been in an epic on-again, off-again relationship with Harvey Pauls the whole time. At least up until a month ago when she swore it was over for good.

Neil grins. "Come to the party and see for yourself."

Whoa. "So, the answer is good enough that she's letting you take her out again. Way to go, man."

"I'm not actually taking her." He shrugs. "She's already going with her sister. But we'll see each other there."

Uh-oh. My Spidey senses start to tingle. "Neil."

He shakes his head. "I know what you're thinking, but she's not stringing me along."

Yep. He knows exactly what I'm thinking. "I don't think she's doing it on purpose."

God help me if I suggest Neil's perfect angel might not be quite as perfect as his big, open heart wants to believe.

"Is she still talking with Harvey? Seeing him?"

It's the question Neil never wants me to ask. But I gotta. If for no other reason than to keep him from getting his head so far in the clouds that when he inevitably falls, it isn't quite so bad.

"Fuck you, man." He shoves a hand through his hair and walks farther down the aisle where he picks up a net and looks me in the eye... and then pointedly puts it back in the wrong spot.

Fucker.

But now I feel like a dick. "Hey, I'm sorry. I just don't want to see you get hurt." Again.

I know what heartbreak feels like, and watching my oldest friend race toward it scares the shit out of me.

He nods. Shakes his head. Then turns and socks me on the shoulder to show we're good. "Fine. Make it up to me. Come to the party. See how it is with Judy. And who knows, maybe you'll even score some tail yourself."

Right. That's not gonna happen, and we both know it. "Look, I can't miss practice. I'm the captain, and we've got a match on Tuesday." I take the net and move it back to where it belongs. Wipe a smudge from the shelf and try not to think about Neil, alone, watching the girl he loves making up with her ex.

Shit.

"But how about I come by after?"

2

Trevor

Even with the open windows and warm evening breeze blowing through, Danny's small bungalow smells faintly of fresh paint and cardboard. The few pieces of furniture—including a couch I'm ninety percent sure I crashed on once at his mom's house—have been pushed against the walls to open the space up for what looks like most of our high school class.

I've been reeling since I walked past the "Sold" sign on the front lawn an hour ago. I knew it would be weird coming back and seeing everyone I went to high school with looking and acting more like grown adults than the kids they were when I left. What I wasn't expecting is all the ways it's the same.

Kelsey Pinsky is still hanging on Jerry Noble's arm,

only instead of his class ring on her hand, it's a modest diamond.

Sue Humphries still has the most contagious laugh around.

Bill Waller and Dex Leighton are still manning the bar, but instead of the six-pack abs they sported when they played football, the guys look like they swallowed a pony keg apiece.

Gail Woo and Mary Trayner are still the go-to source for all things gossip around the lakes. A responsibility they take seriously, as evidenced by the way they cornered me the second they walked in.

"But it's just you? No family or girlfriend in tow?" Gail asks, smoothing her jet black ponytail over one shoulder and not even bothering to disguise the fishing expedition.

"Nah, but Tammy's married with a baby down in Illinois." I pull out my phone, flashing my favorite picture of her and Dominic on the lock screen. "She's about halfway between Springfield and Chicago, and my mom has a place in the town over."

The women exchange patient looks, and Mary changes tactics. "So, are you going to be playing with the Slayers again next season?"

Wouldn't I like to know.

Getting called up to fill Ben Boerboom's spot when he ended up on IR through the end of the season gave me enough ice time to make an impression. Show management what I've got and how I can contribute to the team racking up wins.

But Boomer's cleared to play again and, by all accounts, he's been busting ass to get game ready.

Where that leaves me? I have no idea.

But this is a party, so I laugh like it's all good and I haven't got a care in the world. "Sure hope so."

Mary winks, eyes sparkling as she leans in close enough that I think she's maybe trying to give me a peek down her halter. "I bet the girls are swarming."

They are. Not that it matters to me.

I could say that, tell her the truth. The temptation is there, but even two states away and surrounded by the people I spent a good chunk of my teens with, I can't share the reason why I have no interest in puck bunnies.

Ironic, considering four years ago I was a stone's throw from laying it all out there for the world to see.

One night with Cam, and I thought that was it. I'd found what I was looking for, that piece of me I hadn't even realized I was missing.

One week, and I was ready to change my life. Turn my plans upside down. Give up everything if that's what it took to hold on to him, to us.

Two weeks, and it was over. After being ready to tell the world, I blew out of town without a single soul knowing what had happened between us. That I wasn't the same guy I'd been before. That my life, my heart, were changed forever, written over in indelible ink by a man who wanted to erase us.

Christ, it shouldn't still hurt.

I blink, shaking the past off as best I can and realizing the girls are still waiting for a response. So I fall back on the one I give any time a reporter is looking for a more personal angle.

"Hockey's where I'm focused right now, so I don't have much time to think about women."

The half-truth makes me uncomfortable, as always. And even knowing I don't owe anyone an explanation, something about being back here... Hell, it's like there's this itch begging me to do now what I couldn't do then. Trust my friends with who I really am and share that while I'm not dating now, until two months ago, I was in a serious relationship with a man I thought I loved.

Thing is, I'm so used to protecting my ex's secret that even all these months later and with everything that happened with Leo, I'm afraid that sharing my own truth might shine a spotlight on his.

At some point, I'm going to have to figure it out, but as of now, Leo's fear of people connecting the dots between us is enough for me to keep my heart to myself.

I take a swallow of my beer and search the crowd. Cataloging names and faces, I'm painfully aware of the one I haven't seen yet.

Gail must notice I've checked out and waves her

hand through the space between us like she's brushing my worries away. "Forget next season."

Mary nods, her smile spreading. "Who knows, Trev, maybe you'll find a happily ever after right here in your hometown."

She juts her chin toward the front door, and I nearly choke.

Because that's Cam Dorsey holding it open.

Holy hell, the sight of him sends a jolt of electricity through me, straining my heart and seizing my lungs. Making me ache as I take in the hard-cut cheekbones and strong, square jaw, the dark hair with that still-damp hint of unruly wave. The T-shirt molded over painfully sexy shoulders that somehow look even broader than they did when he was captain of the swim team, and a chest so built it ought to come with a hard-hat warning.

Cam looks *good*.

But once my brain slingshots back from taking inventory of all the ways this man has improved with age, I realize Gail isn't pointing to Cam at all.

She's pointing to Laura Jansen, and that pleasure-pain overload in my system shifts into something uneasy.

"Laura's back, huh?" The petite brunette was one of the few people I kept in touch with when I left. Or rather she kept in touch with me. For a while.

"Uh-huh." Gail's tone has my gut tensing. "And a little birdie told me she's excited to see you too."

Excited? Am I?

Laura is a great person. A sweetheart. I should be pumped to see her.

But there's a history between us. A will-they, won't-they past I was hoping four years apart would close the book on. Unfortunately, the gleam in Gail's eyes tells me she's hoping for a reunion on par with *Bennifer 2.0*, and that is not happening.

I look back to the door where Laura's giving Cam a big hug. Both are smiling wide.

It shouldn't make me jealous. It's *nuts* to be jealous, but seeing those two so natural and easy together when it won't be that way with me sucks.

Especially since one of them is the reason nothing happened with the other.

"Geez, stare any harder?" Gail sings as Mary nods enthusiastically beside her. "Trust me, there's *nothing* between Laura and Cam. I know you've been gone a while, but—"

"Gulls, man, no way!" a gruff voice bellows, catching the attention of most of the party. One of the guys from the hockey team, I think, but my focus is still riveted to the front door. To the former state champ with the hair I remember sifting my fingers through, standing inches taller than anyone in the place.

Cam's head snaps up, his brows buckling as our eyes meet across the room. And yeah, that look is not screaming happy to see me. Figured he wouldn't be.

I'm the asshole who knows his secret. But then he knows mine too.

Still stings.

Before I can even acknowledge him, a couple burly, inked-up arms wrap around me from behind, hoisting me off my feet. "Gulls!"

"There's only one fucker big enough to throw me around." I laugh past my constricted lungs.

"Just sweepin' you off your feet, Princess." Chase Crane guffaws, setting me back on the ground and then hauling me into another bear hug.

"Chase, good to see you, man." The guy's been working construction and somehow managed to double in muscle mass over the past four years. "What the hell has Sandy been feeding you?"

I intentionally use his mother's first name, falling back on the teasing we used to give him about him having the hottest mom on the hockey team. "She still talk about me much?"

Rubbing a hand over his grin, he gives me a slow shake of his ash blond head. If we were sharing ice, I'd have all but guaranteed myself a trip into the boards for that one. Worth it, though.

We catch up a while, me doing my damnedest not to let on that I'm tracking a certain swimmer's every step, smile, and interaction. Waiting to see if he's tracking me.

Spoiler alert: he's not.

More guys from the team get in on the conversation. And damn, I'm surprised how much it feels like coming home.

Of course, Wildren isn't home.

It's a town I left years ago. It's nice to visit. But there's no going back to what this place was to me. Or even what it might have been.

Chase is still giving me a play-by-play of the Wildren High hockey highlights from last season when a head of chestnut curls ducks under my arm and I'm caught in the feminine squeeze of Laura's hold.

"Trevor Gulbrandsen, you sly dog, sneaking into town without calling me," she chides with a warm laugh.

"Hey, thought that was you coming in," I say, hugging her back.

Chase juts his chin at me, flashing a wink before signaling to the group that they're all going for a beer and will be back in a few.

Wow. Not awkward at all.

"Congrats on the degree." I take a step back, still smiling. "What was it, accounting?"

Her eyes light up as she squeezes me again. "Holy buckets, I can't believe you remembered that! Or that I ever thought accounting was for me. I switched to early childhood education."

"A teacher? That's awesome, Laura. You got a gig lined up or still feeling things out?"

She laughs and rests a hand on my chest as she

peers up at me like I just climbed a tree to rescue a kitten. "Same Trevor. Such a sweetie. I've actually got an offer for a full-time position in the fall over in Carver."

"Nice. Must feel good knowing you've got a spot." Not that I'm jealous. The fact that I don't know where I'll be is good. It means I've still got a shot at moving up. Playing between the Orators and Slayers is a good thing... even if it sometimes feels like there's no place I belong at all.

"Yes. I'm lucky." She wags her head, giving up a little sigh. "I am."

There's obviously something else. "But?"

"But Carver's three towns over." She scrunches her nose in that cute way she's always had. "I went to college thirty minutes from home. I don't know, I guess there's a part of me that feels like it might be fun to broaden my horizons some. Have a bit more *adventure*. Excitement. You know?"

"Sure. I get that." I also get that her hand hasn't left my chest and there's something in this prolonged eye contact that's conveying she wouldn't mind if that adventure happened with me.

Again, I find myself searching out Cam and the memories of him every minute in this town seems to unearth.

I'm guessing he isn't a guy after some adventure and excitement, because he hasn't glanced over once since he saw I was here.

But I can't stop looking. His nose is still blade straight. He's dressed in a solid T-shirt with brown cargo shorts that are somehow just that much more understated than what most everyone else has on. There's no ring on his finger— that I can see, anyway.

He came alone. Not that it matters.

Laura gives me a nudge and asks, "Right?"

Shit. She was talking.

"Sorry, Laura. Been a long day of driving. What were you asking?"

She laughs like it's funny instead of putting me on blast like I deserve. The least I can do is pay attention to what this woman— *this friend* —I haven't seen in forever is saying.

"No, nothing... I'm so sorry. I didn't realize you got here today! Uff-da. Are you even up for all these people tonight?"

She's sorry?

"I—"

"If you're wiped, I could drive you home." She bites the corner of her lip, peering up at me through her lashes. "We could have a beer at your place. Talk and catch up some... in private?"

Ehh, shit.

Cam

For four years I've been wondering whether I made a mistake. If I should have trusted in something that felt like it was too good to be true instead of running away like the scared kid that I was.

A handful of times I've broken down and scoured the Internet for any hint that Trevor Gulbrandsen's arrow might not be shooting quite as straight as everyone assumed... but I've never seen even a hint of him following through on that promise he made me out on the lake.

He said he wasn't scared.

That he didn't need to hide.

I know there have been women. I'm not proud of the sites I had to log into to find out, but even playing primarily on the farm team, Trevor draws enough attention to have a smattering of casual encounters show up on the boards.

Not a lot. Hell, there were only three that I found. All women without even a whisper of a man.

But in case that wasn't enough, seeing Laura Jansen tucked up under Trevor's arm, her tits mushed against his side, and this epic eye-lock they have going clears it up for me.

I swallow hard and force my eyes back to Neil and Judy.

At least someone didn't get blindsided tonight. Judy might have shown up separately, but since I got here, she hasn't taken her eyes off my buddy once. And despite having been in love with this girl and captain of the simp squad for most of his life... he's not actually drooling or trying to snip a lock of her hair or doing any of the thousand desperate things I wouldn't put past the sad sap. He's just... having fun. And so is she.

Something I'm not about to get in the way of just because I can barely fucking breathe knowing that Trevor is back in town. So it's time to vamoose. "Hey, man, thanks for getting me out tonight, but I'm beat. Are you cool if I take off?"

He legit can barely peel his eyes off Judy when he clears me to bail. It puts a smile on my face that holds up until I get outside and take a heavy breath as I walk to my truck.

She's old enough to need a key to start and doesn't connect to a phone or any other device, but she's reliable and gets me where I'm going. So I try to treat her right in return. Keep her clean, tune her up, give her a minute before I ask her to get me the fuck away from my greatest heartbreak.

While I wait for her engine to warm up, I look back to the house. And just my luck, there in the front window, Trevor bows his head down to Laura's.

A proposition for her ears only? She tilts her head back and smiles before taking his hand and guiding him toward the door.

3

Cam

I shouldn't be swimming in the lake tonight. My body was spent after practice, but after the party and seeing Trevor? The rhythmic cut of my arms through the water, more meditation than exercise, is all that's keeping me sane.

For all these years, I just sort of liked to think of Trevor as *out there*. A *maybe*. And tonight he went from a rare fantasy I try not to indulge in... to a hard *no*.

Because he's back, but he didn't call. He didn't reach out or stop by the store.

He didn't do anything but show up and put a smile on the face of a girl who has been waiting for him forever. So, good for her. Good for them.

My arms pull through the cool water, my breath drawing every third burning stroke.

It doesn't matter that he's back. It doesn't change anything.

I swim through the darkness, listening to the water and my breath, the sounds of being inside my head.

Breathe, two, three. Breathe, two, three. Breathe, two, three.

Keeping an eye on the shore, I watch for Outlook Rock and then follow the inlet that wouldn't be visible without the light of the full moon. The water changes, calming, and I look up to find the ten square feet of floating dock that is my turning-around point.

In the mornings, I circle it once and head straight home, but tonight? Hell, apparently, I haven't had enough torture. So instead, I plant my hands on the weather-worn boards and propel myself up—

"Fucking wha—"

The startled shout followed by the rocking of the raft have me splashing back into the water mid-breath. I come up hacking so hard I'm probably only catching about a third of the profanities spilling from above in a stream so steady, my next cough turns into a laugh as I push my goggles off and try to choke out an apology.

"Jesus, *Cam*?"

Meaty shoulders and a head in silhouette come into view as a muscular arm thrusts out, locking with mine.

It's not him. It can't be him. Not here.

Except I know the deep timbre of that voice. And while the blond is muted by the night, there's something as familiar about the way the overlong mess falls around those heavy cheekbones as what's happening in my chest.

"Trev?"

That head above me starts a slow, disbelieving shake. "Holy shit, man, you scared ten fucking years off my life."

And before I can think too much about it, the grip on my forearm tightens, and Trevor hauls me up onto the platform like I'm some ninety-pound, top-of-the-pyramid cheerleader instead of six-foot-four of reasonably solid dude. It's nuts.

My ass hits the wood, and the balmy night air warms my skin.

I take a breath and man up, forcing myself to wipe the lake from my eyes and look back to see who else is on this derelict swim dock I've always thought of as mine, or *ours*.

Only there's no girl trying to keep decent, just the man who got away, standing a few feet back... looking more than a little uneasy.

Shit. "Hey, sorry, man. I didn't know anyone was out here."

What the hell is he doing here?

But then, I glance up at the house and see what I missed swimming in. The warm glow of lights cutting through the trees of a property that, to the best of my knowledge, has been unoccupied for the last two years.

"I— I rented it from Finch for a month this summer." He lets out a strained laugh and takes a step closer, which still leaves half a dozen feet between us.

"Cool. That's great." I grip the back of my neck, hating the way every awkward second is systematically stripping away a memory so precious to me, I can barely breathe through it. "Let me get out of your way, here." I swallow. "Now that I know you're here, I'll swim in the other direction."

I slide my feet over the side, the cool water doing little to ease the burn of too many things within me. I'm about to drop back into the lake when a warm hand meets my shoulder before abruptly pulling back.

"You don't have to go. Yet. I mean, you could hang out. Catch up a little." He takes a quick breath that has me slowly turning around. "Didn't get a chance to talk to you at the party."

Resisting the urge to ask what happened with Laura, I shrug. "Too many people for me after a long day."

He clears his throat and steps closer, and I swear there's a shift in the air around us. He gestures to my right. "Mind if I?"

"It's your dock," I say, aiming for light, but my nerves make it come off kind of dickish. So I quickly add, "But yeah. Take a load off."

There's a glint of teeth like maybe he's smiling, and then that big hockey body that is definitely bigger than it was the last time I saw it— touched it —drops down beside me, leaving an ambiguous space between us.

It's not close enough to touch. Not a come-on, that's for sure. But not so far it feels like he's making a point either. He's just there, a few inches away, on the dock where we had our first kiss four— or maybe four *million* —years ago.

And that's got to be why he wants me to stay.

This spot is *private*. Safe. It's the perfect place for a pro athlete with a career on the rise to ask if I'd mind keeping that one time he dipped a toe into the rainbow under wraps.

When he opens his mouth though, it's not to beg for the privacy I'd give him whether he asked for it or not.

Trevor

"HOW'VE YOU BEEN, MAN?" I ask, going for casual like my heart isn't still giving me the Shake Weight treatment, and I wasn't just lying here asking myself *again* if I'd made a monumental mistake coming back.

God, he looks good.

Like some kind of aquatic god with lake water running in rivulets from his hair. Poseidon... if he were twenty-two and wearing a criminally hot, thigh-cut Speedo with a pair of clear goggles clutched in his fist.

He also looks a little confused, like he might have been expecting me to say something else. But what are you supposed to say to the first guy who blew your mind and changed your life forever... then told you goodbye?

No idea, man.

But I try again, because he's here. Swimming right out of my damn thoughts.

And self-destructive or not, I don't want him to go.

"Heard you're still working with your dad." Yeah, I might have asked when I realized he'd left the party while I was letting Laura down in private. "You happy?"

He takes a beat and then relaxes into the question, leaning back on those straight, powerful arms.

"Yeah, I am. To both questions. I actually spent two years at the U and then moved to an online program when my dad needed surgery."

"Oh damn, how's he doing?"

"It took him a while to get up to speed after, but he's good now, thanks. And he's got a shiny new hip out of it that we're hoping will last him through the back nine."

There's no bitterness in the way Cam says it, so I mean it when I tell him I'm glad to hear it.

I know he's close to his dad. Four years ago, protecting that relationship meant more to him than the freedom to be who he was. And, judging from the tone of his voice, there aren't any hard feelings.

No regrets. Not from his side anyway.

Me?

Hell, I'm just trying not to notice the moonlight contouring the lines of Cam's well-defined body in shades of silver and blue. Or how low his suit sits on his hips. How being this close to him settles something inside me, even while it turns so many other things upside down.

But Cam made it clear before I left, there wasn't room for *us* in his life. And as far as I can tell, he's good with how things have turned out.

So what am I doing here, practically begging this guy who just accidentally swam back into my life to stay a few more minutes?

I might have an idea, but before I can think too much about it, he juts his chin at me.

"I've gotta ask. What brings you back here?"

Makes sense he'd want to know. It's not like my roots run deep. We only lived here about five years, and while they were good ones, when I left to play hockey, Mom and Tammy followed.

"When I was playing in Springfield, I didn't really mind sticking around during the off-season. I had friends, a roommate." A relationship. "But uh... when I started getting called up"— I shake my head, hating that I still feel it in my chest — "There was some jealousy. Lost some friends over it."

"Trev, I'm sorry."

I shrug. "Roommate was one of them. And until I

know for sure where I'll be starting the season—
Chicago or Springfield —doesn't make sense to find
another place down south just yet."

"Crazy life," he mutters, staring out at the lake.

I nod. "Guess I had a lot of good memories here.
One night last month, my sister found Finch on Facebook, and everything kind of came together from
there."

"So you might be playing for Chicago now?" He
turns, square jaw resting on his shoulder. "Like a
permanent thing?"

If only.

"Not quite. Training camp plays into things. But it
sounds like management liked how I played while
Boomer was out. Enough that my agent's saying they
might want to try me for a couple games to start the
season, just to see. Doesn't mean I'll stay there."
Doesn't mean they won't change their mind
completely.

"Doesn't mean you won't," he says, like he knows
something I don't.

"True. Still. Lots of question marks." And no end to
them in sight.

Cam takes a deep breath. Even in the darkness,
there's something thoughtful in the slope of his shoulders and angle of his head. Something beautiful about
this man beneath the night sky.

"It's got to be rough having so much uncertainty,"

he says. And damn, I need to stop staring like a creeper.

"Yeah, but I get to play. And that makes it worth it."

A smile. "Ah... the trade-offs."

"Always, right?" I expect him to chime in with a hearty agreement, because if anyone should get it, I imagine it's him.

"Sorry about your friends not supporting your achievement, man. Sounds like you're better off without them. But even so, that's bullshit and it's gotta suck."

I laugh. "That it does." In ways I'm afraid to talk to even him about.

Instead, I ask about our friends from high school, wanting to hear the same updates I already got at the party, but in his words. His rich voice. I ask about his dad's store and school and swimming, which is now water polo for him. I ask the polite questions old friends ask, skimming the moonlit surface between our lives without delving into the inky waters below.

Without telling him the things that really matter to me or asking him the same. Things like whether he's found love, or if he ever thought about me the way I've thought about him. Because I don't want to risk crossing a line with Cam that might make him shut me out again.

We end up laughing about the time Randy Harris smuggled his new puppy into school, and how all the teams came together to hide him.

"Football, band, chess, and debate." He's got that one arched-brow thing going, and combined with his crooked smile, it's taking everything I've got not to lean in and touch him. "Hockey, newspaper, and swimming. I don't even know who coordinated the effort, but we had that puppy daycare running out of the west bathroom for the better part of a week."

"Pretty sure we got busted on day three. Sylvia Cortez was allergic and had to go to the nurse with asthma and hives."

He snorts. "She married one of the Lacher brothers. Sylvia, I mean. Baby number three is on the way."

I let out a whistle. "Three? Jesus. I can't even commit to a dog."

He laughs and then slowly, the laughter fades into a silence that stretches and pulls at this thing between us.

This thing I know better than to give in to.

Him, too.

"It's getting late." He leans back and rocks up to stand.

Shit, shit, shit.

He stretches out his shoulders beneath the moonlight, powerful arms swinging in a few mesmerizing arcs. "See you around, yeah?"

I get to my feet and nod too, looking away so I don't stare at his flawless body.

God, his ass in that suit.

He doesn't hesitate, just takes a couple fluid steps

and does a shallow dive before popping up. I need to stop him. Say something.

"Hey, Cam."

He rolls onto his back to face me, arms barely moving at the surface.

"I won't—" I clear my throat and try again. I can't let him worry about me outing him. "You know, I won't say anything about what happened with us. That last summer." It's too dark to read his features, but I— Shit, maybe I shouldn't have mentioned it at all. "Cam?"

"Yeah, I wasn't worried. But I won't either." He's pulling away, his arms slicing back overhead, one and then the other. "Not that it would make a difference if you did. Everyone knows I'm gay."

The dock rocks, or maybe it's just me. But suddenly my chest is doing something almost violent. "Wait, what?"

He stops with a short laugh, holding up a hand, because I'm balanced at the edge, a breath away from diving in after him.

"Whoa, Trev. Settle. Don't worry. You're secret's safe with me, man. Always was. Always will be." And he's on the move. One stroke, two, and then without breaking his rhythm, he rolls onto his stomach and swims off into the darkness.

4

Cam

Running my hands over my face, I listen to the chime of my phone alarm gently increase in volume. I don't want to get up.

I don't want to start another day knowing that Trevor is back in town. I don't want to be looking for him around every corner, thinking I see him in every crowd, and if it actually is him, making sure no one picks up on that weirdly intense vibe between us.

But most of all, I don't want to get caught in the same whirlpool of regret I lived in when he left after high school.

Because I had my chance.

He'd taken my hand that last day while the house he lived in with his mom and sister was emptied into a moving truck, and told me he was all in. That we didn't have to hide. Trevor wanted me. And anyone who didn't like it could screw off.

I'd thought about my dad. The store. Everyone I knew and the life I was terrified to lose... and then I told him I couldn't. I wouldn't.

The big, tough captain of the hockey team stood before me with tears in his beautiful blue eyes and begged me to change my mind. To give us a chance. He swore no one had to know. That if I wasn't ready, we could keep it a secret. He'd stay. Get a job. That we could find a way.

I wanted him. But I wasn't ready. I'd been too scared to trust. Him. Myself. The people I loved most in this world.

Turns out, most of my friends and family were pretty awesome when I told them.

But Trev? Okay, who knows what would have happened if I'd said yes that last night instead of getting in my truck and driving straight through until morning so there was no way I could get back before he left.

Maybe if I'd given us a chance, he would have been all in the way he promised. Or maybe he would have realized within a few hours or days that we weren't worth risking his dreams over—

Fuck. I press the heels of my hands against my eyes and rub.

This kind of speculation is exactly what I don't want to start my damn day with.

My life is good. It's everything I said I wanted. And his life just keeps getting better. I've seen him play. No way are the Slayers sending him back down.

And he's not out.

It's that simple.

All I need to do is stay away from him and both our lives will keep on going just the way we want them to.

Easy. Last night was a moment of weakness. Okay, more like two hours of weakness. Followed by another of sitting in the dark, watching all the Internet clips of Trevor I could find on my laptop.

I throw my legs out of bed, stretch the muscles that got twice their anticipated workout yesterday, and get ready for work. I'm already running late, so there's no time for coffee or breakfast, only a record-breaking shower before I hop in the truck and start to drive.

I'm making a bigger deal of him being back than I need to.

Seriously, I need to turn my focus back to the here and now. The town I love. The natural beauty that is literally surrounding me with the deep woods and a lush canopy of maples, cedar, balsams, and birch so thick the warm, golden sun can only sneak through for a peek here and—

What the hell?

I brake to a crawl as I approach the completely jacked hottie jogging shirtless up my road. The man who isn't a permanent fixture in this landscape but fits in like he never left.

Trev's wide smile is directed at me. He waves and starts to walk, pushing thick fingers through a mess of untamed blond waves I really shouldn't be thinking about getting my fingers into... *pulling*. Sweat drips down the hard-packed terrain of his chest and layered abs, soaking into a pair of gray sport shorts that don't leave nearly enough to the imagination.

And as if all that mouthwatering hotness isn't torture enough, *he hasn't shaved*. This man's morning-after stubble glinting in the early sun is like my personal kryptonite.

I should keep driving, flash a smile, and roll right past. But glutton for punishment that I am, I pull to a stop beside him and lean out my open window with a grin. "I don't see you once in four years, and now this is three times in twenty-four hours. We've got to stop meeting like this."

For a minute, he looks like he's going to say something, but instead he takes a few seconds to catch his breath as he looks around. Then, "Pretty up through here."

"Yeah, it is." Even more so with him around for the next month.

"You a runner?" he asks with a jut of his chin, those blue eyes coming back to mine.

Only from you.

I grip the back of my neck, reminding myself not to

get excited. It's not like he was going to ask me along or something. "Not really. I get my cardio in the pool."

"And lake." A dimple pops in his cheek, and suddenly I've got to shift in my seat.

Were these jeans this tight when I put them on?

"And the lake," I agree with a laugh that feels like it comes from some deeper place inside me than I knew I had. "I'm not much for land sports."

"Yeah." He scrubs a wide hand over that rough-cut jaw, and holy shit, the way he's looking at me, those hot eyes dragging from my eyes to my hair to my mouth... my chest.

It's almost like— No, that can't be right.

I swallow hard, looking at the steering wheel, the side mirror. Him.

Get it together, man.

"Seriously, though, aren't you supposed to be on break? I slept in to the last possible second this morning, forgoing my shot at a decent cup of coffee so I could get an extra ten minutes." And then I remember that I'm on my way to work. "*Oh shit!* I really did oversleep. I've gotta go, or I'm going to be late."

Trevor steps back from the car with a grin. "Not on my watch. Get out of here."

Taking my foot off the break, I start to roll. "Have a good run."

He shrugs. "Basically done. Just saw you swim off this way last night and was curious where your place was."

It takes a second, but then the truck jerks to a stop with an embarrassing screech. "You were looking for me?"

That fucking smile. "Don't you have somewhere you're supposed to be?"

～

Trevor

WHAT THE HELL am I doing? Last week, I would have sworn the only reason I was coming back here was to hide out from the world and be alone. Now?

One glimpse of Cam and my heart started in on the aerobics.

A couple hours of talking, and all the plans I thought were rock-solid suddenly feel rocky instead.

A few minutes this morning and— well, no turning back now.

I shoulder through the front door of Dorsey Outfitters, looking up when an old-fashioned bell sounds above my head and then taking in the rest of the store with a growing sense of unease.

Not what I was expecting.

In all the time I lived in Wildren, I never had a reason to come in here. My mom didn't hunt or fish, so it wasn't how I grew up. All my time went to hockey. And while Cam worked here, we weren't the kind of friends where I'd show up at his job to hang out or make plans. So I'm not prepared for the sheer size of the place, the warm, lodge-like atmosphere, or that, thirty minutes after opening, it's already hopping.

But apparently Dorsey's is where the senior sect hangs out.

There are no less than a dozen old-timers ranging in age from I'm guessing sixty to ninety. They're parked on long couches watching some bass fishing program like the last episode of *Pam & Tommy* just dropped. They're pouring refills at a coffee station with a tray of mismatched ceramic mugs and a warehouse-sized canister of powdered creamer. Two of them are leaning against the counter shooting-the-shit style over a copy of what I'd bet is the *Gazette*. And behind the counter, in that torturously hot, fitted black polo with the store logo over his left pec is Cam.

He's nodding attentively to this shrunken raisin of a man who looks to be telling some kind of big-fish story based on the slow-motion gesturing happening over there.

"Gullsy, that you?" A burly guy with a gray buzz cut slaps his knee from the couch.

Behind the counter, Cam straightens.

I raise a hand in greeting, and the old guy gives up a wheezing laugh. "Just this morning Missy was telling me that Cheryl heard from Pastor Craig you were back in town."

Face heating, I nod. "Yes, sir. Back for a month."

There's a chorus of croaked greetings and

comments about my last game with the Slayers. It's nice but also makes me feel more than a little conspicuous.

Eventually, I make my way over to the counter where Cam's standing in a wide-legged stance, arms crossed over his broad chest, a curious smirk on his handsome, clean-cut face.

"So much for my plan to quietly drop some coffee by for you. Half the town's in here." I look back to where most everyone's attention has returned to fishing. "Didn't realize this was such a hot spot."

"That it is. Is one of those for me?" he asks, nodding toward the heavy-duty paper cups in my hand.

Trying to be cool, I hold one out. "Felt bad about you missing your coffee window. Though I guess you've got plenty here."

The corner of his mouth twitches as he waves me closer. I lean over the counter, and he meets me halfway. There's a wash of his breath against my skin, and I close my eyes against the sensation, afraid of what they'd reveal.

"It's *decaf*. They don't know, but we've been making both pots with the same stuff since before I was born. A deal Gramps made with one of the wives forever ago, and we've stuck with."

"Whoa." I pull back a couple inches, as far as I can willingly make myself go. "And you trust me with this state secret?"

His laugh is low and warm, the same one I remember from when we were paired up for biology lab in high school, the one that drew me in with a force I didn't understand. But made me curious just the same.

"What?" he asks before taking a sip and then rocking back on his heels with an almost pornographic moan. Or maybe it was standard appreciation and the fact that I haven't gotten any for damn near six months is starting to screw with my head.

"Just thinking about the first time I noticed your laugh." I say it quietly, but his brows still go up and his eyes shift from me to the crowd behind us.

I know. *Careful.*

If I don't want people to know, I shouldn't say things like that. I shouldn't find reasons to be jogging by his house or bringing him coffee at work. But that's the thing... Cam makes me want people to know. He makes me want another shot at that thing we barely had a chance to skim the surface of the first time around.

But while I'm winding up to send caution into the wind, he's taking a step back from the counter.

That soaring feeling in my chest starts to sink until he holds up a finger for me to wait.

Ducking into an open doorway at the far end of the glass top, he clears his throat. "Dad? Can you handle refills on the coffee for a few? I'll hit inventory this afternoon."

There's a muffled response, and then Mr. Dorsey emerges from the back with a stack of paperwork and a laptop. There's no mistaking the family resemblance. The fall of dark hair and square-cut jaw, the broad build on a lean frame. "Where you off to?"

"Just out back. Come and get me if there's a run on the register."

His dad snorts and waves him off.

And then I'm following Cam through the back of the store and out to a narrow strip of fenced-in grass with a shaded picnic table in the center. It's private and quiet enough that the only sound I hear is the rustling of the breeze through the trees.

I rub the back of my neck. "Hey, sorry about showing up like that. I shouldn't—"

"I'm glad you did." He drops onto one bench and signals for me to take the opposite side. "Needed the coffee." He wags his head with one of those half-smiles I can't seem to look away from. "It's not bad seeing you again, either."

Heat floods my cheeks, and after a minute of studying my cup, I ask, "So everyone inside... knows?"

"That I'm gay? Yeah, they know." He watches me a second, running his teeth over his bottom lip. "But if you're worried they'll make an assumption about you showing up today, don't."

I nod slowly, thinking about it for a moment. *Really thinking.* And the I meet his eyes. "I'm not."

5

————

Cam

"You're not." He's not worried? What does that mean?

Trevor must see the gears turning in my head. He sets his cup down and rests his forearms on the table. The breath he takes before going on has me holding my own.

"Four years ago, I didn't see you coming." He looks away, almost shy. "Yeah, I knew there was something about you. Even before that night, I couldn't keep my eyes off you. I told myself it was one athlete's appreciation of another. That I only knew the dip and rise of every muscle on your body because I wanted that level of fitness myself. That I gravitated toward you because our ambitions matched."

"Trev." I stare, stunned by the unguarded words. But I shouldn't be— it's how he's always been with me.

He gives me a sheepish smile. "I thought the pull in my chest and gut was because I was just more comfortable around guys like me. And when I felt that pull even lower, I passed it off as teen horniness. I mean, I was attracted to women. I dated them, casually. So the reality of that attraction sort of snuck up on me. But once I understood it, it was a relief."

Christ, how am I sitting here with this man again? How is he telling me these things that tear at my heart and make it hard for me to breathe, that touch on a connection that feels as fresh now as it did then? These things that wreck me.

"Except I wasn't ready." I let out a humorless laugh. "It didn't matter that I very much understood my attraction to you. I knew I was gay. I was interested in dudes from the start. And the few girls I took out... well, let's just say I'm glad I'm not still trying to sell the straight thing." I shake my head and give him a truth I wasn't planning to share. "I wish I'd been brave enough to come out about it sooner."

He shakes his head, squinting into the distance.

"You had your reasons. And coming here today, seeing what you were afraid of losing, I get those reasons even more now." His eyes meet mine. "But when I left, I didn't."

Even now, I remember the look on his face from

that last night, the plea and pained disbelief when I rejected him. It haunts me. "I'm sorry."

For him. For me. For everything that fear cost me.

He shakes his head. "Don't. You have *nothing* to apologize for. Not a single thing. If anything, I owe you my thanks."

I raise a brow, and he shrugs one solid shoulder.

"You helped me figure out some pretty significant truths about myself. Things I hadn't recognized on my own. I mean it. And for a short time, it was just... Perfect. So, thank you."

I nod, but there's something I still don't get. "Can't believe I'm actually going to admit this, but I looked you up a few times."

The corners of his mouth twitch. "What were you looking for?"

"For an *out* hockey player." For the things he told me to be real. It's as far as I can go. As much as I can admit, because there's no way I'm going to tell him that if I found what I was looking for, I'd have hit the gas and driven straight through until I got to him. I'd have begged for a second chance.

Slowly, he nods. "At first, I guess I was kind of torn up and confused. What happened with us felt like a lightning strike. I'd never experienced anything close to it before, and it took a while before I could even think about anyone else. And then..." Tracing an invisible pattern into the worn wood of the table, he lifts a shoulder. "Hell, I'd been so sure about us. And being wrong? It made me doubt things some. Wonder if maybe I'd been wrong about more. If maybe what happened between us was just a fluke."

I rub at the pain in my chest, the soul-deep scar I gave to both of us.

"So you went back to dating girls?"

He lets out a quiet laugh, staring down at his hands. "Let's say, I confirmed that I'm bisexual. I'm physically attracted to women. Been a few nights here and there where something physical was all I wanted. But when it comes to guys, I'm physically *and* emotionally attracted."

My mouth goes dry. "You've had... relationships... with men?"

"Two."

"I didn't see anything." My ears are ringing, and my chest feels like an anvil is parked on it.

"The first lasted a few months but wasn't meant to be. Different lives and directions. Probably a little *too easy* to let go, you know? If it hadn't fizzled, I think we would have been open about the relationship, but he wasn't big on PDA. So while it was happening, no one noticed anything more than a couple guys hanging out now and then."

I try to imagine it but realize I don't want to. Still, I have to know. "The second?"

"The second was almost a year. My ex wasn't out. Isn't out. He said maybe someday, but I went into it with my eyes open. Even so, pretending for all that time is rough, you know?"

But he'd done it. For almost a year.

If I'd believed him. If I'd trusted, maybe we—

I shake my head, because that's a train of thought I don't think I can afford to follow sitting right in front of him. "Is that why it ended?"

He looks away but not before I see the hurt in his eyes. I don't like it.

"There were a lot of reasons. But his not wanting our relationship to be public wasn't really one of them. His cheating on me though... definitely was."

"Trevor, man, I'm so sorry. When did you break up?"

"Officially? Few months ago. But it had been over for a while by then."

About the time he was playing with the Slayers. I want to ask him more about it. But there's no missing the subtle shift in his body language, the way he closes off. Like he's still protecting this jerk.

So I stick to the only question that really matters.

"Are you over him?"

"Him? Yeah. *It?* I want to be, but that kind of betrayal has a way of sticking with you." A breeze blows through, tossing his hair around his face. "What really catches me up, though? The part that I resent the hell out of but can't seem to get past, is this concern that if *I* come out, it changes things for him. Puts his secret at risk."

46

"How do you mean?"

"Everyone knew we were friends. He's terrified if people find out I date guys, they might draw conclusions. That even if they don't know for sure... what if they ask him about me? About whether he knew? How he feels?"

"So now you... what? Feel like you can't?" I reach across the scarred wood and take his hand. I only let myself hold it for a second, just long enough to offer the smallest comfort before giving him back his space. "It's admirable that you want to respect his privacy, but I think you can do that and still live your own life. If anyone asks him about you... he can decide what he wants to say about it."

The look on his face says even if he thinks I'm right he isn't comfortable with it.

Spearing a hand through the overlong mess of his hair, he swings his legs out from the bench to stand. "You know, I've had a hard time making peace with that. Part of me felt like, without a good reason, what's the harm in giving him more time to put some distance between us? But maybe he's had enough time."

Abandoning our coffees on the bench, I rise with him. "What changed your mind?"

His eyes meet mine, and the air in my lungs catches behind everything I'm seeing there.

He steps closer, moving into my space so there's less than a foot separating us. Dappled sunlight plays across his brow, the crooked bridge of his nose, and those brawny shoulders, highlighting one perfect spot and then the next. Making me want to touch, to reach out and wrap my hand around the back of his neck, fist his shirt, and drag him in for a kiss.

Only, I can't fucking move. I can't breathe as he searches my eyes with a helplessness completely at odds with his physical presence. "I saw you again."

"*Trev.*"

In what seems like some kind of slow-motion reality, Trevor reaches for my hand, the backs of his knuckles brushing lightly, tentatively... heating the nerves where our skin touches and sending tiny waves of static up my arm.

His eyes drift to my mouth, and whatever restraint I've built up for this man crumbles to dust. I can't hold back, can't stop myself from closing the distance between us. I graze his lips with a kiss that's nothing like the heated desperation of my fantasies but somehow feels infinitely more potent.

Our eyes meet, and this time, there's nothing helpless in his look. There's no question between us. Emotion I've kept buried so deep for so long surges up in an almost violent eruption, and we come together in a crush, chest to chest, mouths fusing, hands gripping and pulling and— Christ —there's not an inch between us. Not a breath we aren't sharing.

How does this kiss feel more intimate than any sexual act I've ever engaged in?

There isn't a pause or beat or a single second of hesitation as we angle and open, taking and giving, our tongues moving together and sliding against each other. Each spearing thrust making me moan as sensation pierces through me in ways no kiss has before. Or at least not in the past four years.

Our feet aren't as coordinated as our mouths, and suddenly I'm staggering in a tangle of blind steps, Trev's arm locking around me as the outside wall to the stockroom meets my shoulders and his hard body presses into mine... all the way down.

Oh hell, yes. I can feel him thickening against me and—

zzz zzz

"Oh shit," I croak, breaking away even though it nearly kills me to do it.

But my phone's on DND for work, and only one person's texts come through.

"Phone?" Trevor asks with a gruff, breathless laugh.

Our brows are still pressed together, our chests rising and falling like we've just finished back-to-back 1500 frees.

"Yeah, I— Sorry, my dad."

He nods without breaking contact.

zzz zzz

The corner of his mouth tips into a crooked slant that has the blood plummeting out of my head so fast I feel dizzy.

"You should check that." Slowly, he draws the hand that was in my hair down my neck, past my shoulder, over my lats where it rotates so his fingers lead the way, teasing lower to skim the rise of my ass.

My throat goes dry. That crooked smile is too much. Aching for another taste, I lean in, but Trevor matches my movement, drawing back.

"Your *dad*." He slides his hand over my hip, and I can almost feel the phantom tug of him fisting my jeans, but instead, he works that big, slow dragging hand into my pocket and withdraws my phone just as it vibrates again.

Eyes still locked with mine, he hands over the device I'm tempted to use as a longbow target. "I should go."

Terrible idea. "Don't. Just give me a minute to let him know I'm leaving, and—"

His single-step retreat sinks my hopes of taking things back to my place and spending the next twenty-four hours or maybe twenty-four years in bed with this man.

"The store opened less than an hour ago. What's it going to look like when I throw you over my shoulder and skate out of here?"

Hot. Insanely so.

And while I've got Trevor by about two inches,

there's zero doubt in my mind that he could do it. Easily. Throw me on the bed and be on top of me before I bounce. But the smile that fantasy conjures fades when the rest of his words sink in.

What's it going to look like...

"Right. Sorry, I wasn't thinking about people seeing us." I start my own retreat, only I'm already against the building and there's nowhere to go.

Trevor laughs, grabbing my hand and pulling me with him over to the bench where our coffees sit. Handing me mine, he leans in and drops a quick kiss at my jaw before stepping back.

"This might sound crazy, but in this moment... the only person I'm worried about knowing is your dad. Part of me will always think he's the reason I lost you the first time."

I open my mouth, but he lifts the fingers of one hand in a sort of abbreviated stop signal.

"I know, there were a million more factors than him. And I get that he's supportive now. Hell, I'm thrilled about it. But I've been waiting four years to feel like this again. I don't want to risk your dad deciding he doesn't like me for stealing his star employee during work hours." He bites his lip, looking out from beneath the blond hank that keeps falling into his eyes. "Besides, I was thinking maybe we could hang out later."

I brush the hair back before I can think about

whether it's really appropriate, loving the softness of the strands between my fingers. "Tonight?"

"Yeah. Like a date, if you're into it. Or if you'd rather—"

"A date." I start nodding like a tool, and a nearly blinding grin breaks across his face. He texts himself from my phone and leans in like he's going to kiss me, but then sways back with a slow shake of his head.

"Better not risk it."

My phone starts to vibrate again, this time with a call. I pick it up. "Sorry, Dad. I'm on my way back in now."

6

Trevor

"A date? Like you're going out in public and holding hands through a candlelit dinner kind of date?"

"I don't know. That's the problem." I put the last handful of socks in the dresser drawer and stow my now empty suitcase in the hall closet. Has it seriously been less than a day since I got here? "I want to take him out, but I ran to the gas station this afternoon and I kid you not, it took forty-five minutes to get out of there. *After* I'd filled up and paid."

Tammy laughs. "I'm jealous. It would be so much fun to see everyone."

"Don't get me wrong. It is. But this is going to be *our* first date. I want to spend it with him, not fielding questions about my life without him."

"You should have stayed at the party longer last night. Then everyone would already be caught up."

Answering with a noncommittal hum, I prop a shoulder against the window and look out through the trees to the water beyond. She might be right, but I wouldn't trade what happened for anything.

"Okay, little brother, here's what you're going to do..."

THE HOURS CREEP by slower than the week leading to Christmas when you're eight. But eventually, I hop in the truck and drive up my lane and back down to Cam's. Our houses look like they were built about the same time and in the same style, but where mine looks like it hasn't been occupied in two years and has the overgrowth to prove it, Cam's is neat as a pin. No branches touch the roof, and the gravel drive is evenly graded, ending in a wide turnabout. From there, a flagstone paver path circles the house with a split that leads to the front porch.

Nerves on par with the first time I stomped down the chute with the Slayers, I walk up to the door and knock. Waiting, I take in the thick, lush lawn with diagonal lines mowed into it and what appears to be a fresh coat of paint on the rail. This is what it looks like to put down roots.

The thought sends an uneasy feeling through my

gut, but then Cam's at the door, looking hot as hell in a dove gray button-down that hugs his impressive biceps and shows off the tapered cut of his torso.

"Hey, sorry, I'm running late," he says, stepping back with a wave at his neatly combed but not quite dry hair. "Delivery showed up as I was closing the store, and I got behind a few minutes."

There's a beat where it's clear he doesn't know what to do with his hands or quite how to greet me.

"No worries and no rush." And then because I'm trying to at least look like I've got some game when my actual *dating* experience with guys is next to nil, I reach for his hip and lean in to drop a quick kiss at his jaw. "You look great... really great."

And that hit of his aftershave mingling with the woodsy scent of his soap and product? *Damn*, it totally does it for me. And now I'm wishing I'd jerked off before I left because I'm at serious risk of sporting wood the whole night.

"Yeah? Thanks," he says quietly. "You too."

When his eyes come up and connect with mine, everything slows and the moment stretches. I feel that same sort of dizzying pull drawing me in, but somehow I manage to step back with only the smallest groan.

Based on the slant of his mouth and the color pushing into his cheeks, he hears it. But I don't think he's going to hold it against me.

"Umm, take your time getting ready. No rush. I'll be in the car."

I don't give him the chance to respond. Just spin on my heel and get the hell out before I do something crazy like back him against another handy wall and drop to my knees for him.

My fingers feel numb as I slide into the driver's seat and start the engine. If I'd hoped for a reprieve to get the situation in my trousers under control, I don't get it. Cam's out of the house within a minute, jogging down the couple stairs from the porch and stepping into the evening sun.

Gorgeous. Definitely should have jerked off.

He climbs in with a hesitant look. "Second thoughts? We don't have to go out if you're not comfortable."

This guy is amazing. But oblivious as to the source of my problem.

"My sister told me not to kiss you before our date." Jesus, I sound like an ass.

One dark brow pushes up. "Tammy? What's she got against kissing?"

"Nothing, if I thought I'd be able to stop."

"Sooo, you didn't think you'd be able to stop?" And the smile he gives me? Embarrassment totally worth it. He bites his bottom lip.

Is he doing it on purpose now?

He reaches across the cab and slides his fingers into the hair at the back of my neck.

Yep. He's definitely doing it on purpose.

I stop breathing, my eyes cutting back to his.

Doesn't Cam realize we're within caveman-hauling distance of his bed?

Don't. Think. About. Beds.

We *have* to make it to the restaurant, so I try to remember what we were talking about. There was something I wanted him to know... Right!

"I didn't want you to wonder"— I clear my throat —"if this was just a hookup. It's not."

"So no kissing at all then?" The way he says it, deep brown eyes dropping to my mouth, just a hint of disappointment in his tone, is killing me. "Not even one?"

The feel of his fingers against my neck is making me stupid. "I really want to take you out."

He nods. "You will. But since I've been thinking about kissing you again since the minute you left the store, maybe we risk it. Set a timer or something."

I've been thinking about kissing him again since I left too. And for the four years before that. Which is why, against my better judgment, I don't resist when he pulls me in. Our mouths meet in a firm press that feels so right, I just lean into the contact, savoring the connection.

He pulls back the barest breath.

"Hey, Google," he mutters. "Set a timer for sixty seconds."

And then we meet again, our mouths rubbing

together in an unhurried kiss that makes my chest ache and my mind spin. We open to each other, our tongues teasing lightly from my mouth to his and back again. It's sweet and hot and all I can think is... *yes*... *this*... and *more*.

I want more than this kiss, more than the single month I'll be living here. Fuck, I want more than a life that can't accommodate anything beyond a career in flux.

Maybe it's that last thought that has my desperation ramping up, because suddenly I can't get close enough. Cam's seatbelt releases a second before mine, and we surge together.

The grip on my neck tightens as we groan into each other. And then I'm pulling at his shoulder while his other hand, wide and strong, slides up my thigh, higher, closer—

Chimes start to sound, and we freeze.

Painfully, I ease back as he turns off the alarm.

Cam's hair isn't quite as neat, but the hint of disarray is sexy as hell, and I can't help but reach up to touch it again.

He smiles, rubbing his hand over his mouth and jaw.

"So, are there any other cockblocking tips big sister bestowed?"

Falling back in my seat, I laugh. We both re-buckle, and I put the truck in gear.

"She told me not to make you dinner at my place for the same reason."

"You cook?" Cam's almost breathless the way he asks, and I make a mental note that our next date will be at my place.

"She told me to take you out of town, but to make sure you know it's not that I don't want people here to see us. It's because I don't want to share you with a bunch of awesome old friends who've been getting to see you on the regular since you were born. I don't want to risk someone mistaking our date as platonic and deciding to join us."

He nods, the corner of his mouth twitching with the smile he doesn't want to set free.

"Trev, do you actually think if they saw us at a table for two, with you dressed like this"— he runs a finger over my linen pant leg, up over my belt, and then flicks the silk of my light blue dress shirt, making me suck in a breath —"they'd think we were just a couple buddies catching up?"

Eyes focused on the road, I shake my head. "I don't know what they'd think. You're the first guy I've ever taken on a real date."

~

Cam

For having zero practice dating, Trevor Gulbrandsen is a natural when it comes to showing a man a good time.

The place he picked is a few towns away, situated on a lake with three walls of windows giving every seat in the dining room an open-air feel and spectacular view. He asks if I'm a "wine guy" and has the waiter help pick out something that will go with our meals.

It's comfortable. Like there's this crazy sense of ease that shouldn't be between us after all this time, with how things ended and the way our lives have moved on since. But I can't remember a conversation ever coming so easily or flowing so naturally from one topic to the next.

And damn, laughing with this man is something else.

He's beautiful to me. And I'm torn between never wanting this dinner to end and pretty desperately wanting to see where it goes next.

I've been on my share of dates. First dates and dates that have happened well into a relationship. But it's never felt like this.

Setting down my silverware, I watch as Trevor wipes his mouth and sets his napkin aside. Something so mundane as using a napkin shouldn't be sexy, but... *so sexy*.

"Thank you for asking me out tonight."

He nods, looking adorably pleased. "I'm glad I did. And hey, four years later, pretty sure this place is way nicer than anything I would have come up with the first time around."

"I'm serious. When you came by Outfitters this morning, there was a part of me that wondered if maybe you came back because you thought I was still in the closet. And that if anything happened, you wouldn't have to worry about it getting out."

He jerks back. "What? No. Cam, I—" He shakes his head and tries again. "I don't know what I thought would happen with you. I— yeah, I wanted to see you. But I was pretty sure you'd be actively avoiding me the whole time I was here. And if you had, I wouldn't have held it against you. I swear."

"You're a good man, Trevor. And no matter what version of my life you walked into, I don't think I'd have a shot in hell at being able to resist you. But in this one, I don't even want to try."

Again he looks away, like he can take a hit from an opposing player on the ice in stride, but a compliment is too much. I'll have to work on that.

Only as soon as the thought crosses my mind, I check it. Because Trevor isn't here to stay. He's here for a few weeks. And then he'll be back in Chicago playing for the Slayers... because I can't believe for a second they'll let him go back down to Springfield.

And then like his thoughts were somehow echoing my own, he meets my eyes. "In this version of my life, things are pretty messy. The only thing I know for certain about my future is that I have four weeks in

Wildren. But beyond that, I—" He searches my eyes, a pain moving into his. "I can't even make plans for myself. I don't know what city I'm going to live in. What team I'm going to play for. And the thing is, as much as that kind of uncertainty sucks, I've got to be grateful for it. Remember how lucky I am and how many guys would do anything to be in my place. This is what I wanted, but there are times when having it is harder than I expected it to be."

"Maybe that's why you came back. Maybe you needed a break from all the worry and waiting for answers. Maybe you just needed something simple for a little while."

I mean it to be reassuring but somehow it isn't.

Trevor nods but then drops his head for a breath. When he looks back up, that buoyancy I was feeling in my chest is replaced by something heavy, resigned. Because we both recognize the truth of it.

"Cam. The way I want you... I don't think this thing between us could ever be *simple*."

7

———

Trevor

The drive back is quiet. But somehow, it's not uncomfortable even after the truth of our situation became obvious. My thoughts bounce between the taste of Cam's kiss, the warm, free sound of his laughter, and what a damn fool I was for coming here when the only thing I know about my life is that this career I've been working toward forever is maybe, possibly, almost within my grasp.

That I nearly sacrificed my chance at the NHL once for this man... only to realize he didn't want me to. He didn't want me at all.

It was more than that.

It was.

I understand. But being back here, feeling myself

falling again before I even realized I'd gotten close to the cliff—

Damn.

I should know better.

I should want to end this date as quickly as possible. Grab that bottle of tequila Lizzo's been saving for me and put us both out of our misery.

But even knowing better, *I don't want this to end.*

Wrapping my hands around the wheel, I hold tight so I don't reach for him.

Another mile, and my time is up. I take a left down his drive, my heart sinking as I pull to a stop in front of his perfect house.

I cut the engine and let myself out while he does the same.

Wind rustles through the trees, muting the rush of waves as we stand facing each other in the moonlight.

"Thank you." I swallow hard. "For letting me take you out and pretend for a few hours that my life was in a place where I could have something like this." Someone like him.

Cam nods, giving me a smile that hurts to look at. "It's nice to be reminded what a good date feels like. And nice to be with you. It's always been that way."

"It has." I lift an arm, inviting him in for a hug because I can't not give him one. And after tonight, there's no telling whether I'll have another chance. I'm supposed to be in town for a month, but the idea of living this close to Cam Dorsey and pretending I don't know what his mouth feels like on mine or how good we could be together if only both our lives and priorities were completely different? It's brutal.

He steps into me, wrapping one arm around my back while giving my shoulder a friendly squeeze with the other. *Ouch.*

I ought to be grateful he's able to be so cool about this, but it feels wrong.

Our chests linger in that half press, his head beside mine. Neither of us moving, like maybe he needs this last contact the same way I do.

Too soon, his hand leaves my shoulder.

That's it.

This is the end.

Except instead of letting me go, by some miracle, he pulls me closer, both arms coming around my back, his hands fisting in my shirt as he buries his face in my neck.

A shock of breath bursts free and then I'm clinging to him with a force that matches his.

"Trevor." He burrows impossibly closer, his voice as rough as I've ever heard it. "I get that it's not as simple as it could be, or even as simple as you need. But maybe... it doesn't have to be that complicated either."

I blink, unable to move or speak or breathe.

"Maybe," he goes on, "if we went into this with our eyes open and no expectations beyond this month—"

"*Cam.*" However he's going to finish that has to

wait. Because my fist is in his hair, and our mouths are slamming together in a demanding crush.

There's more tenderness in my heart for Cam than I have ever felt for another, but this kiss conveys none of it.

This kiss is desperate and hungry.

Deep and aggressive.

This kiss is *everything*.

His tongue is in my mouth, rubbing firm against the press of mine. Our chests and hips bump together as we angle and shift, needing to get closer. Needing more.

"Inside," he commands, fingers caught in my belt, tugging me with him as he backs toward the house.

My hands are on his ass, molding the hard muscle through his pants as he groans into my mouth. Then groans louder when I splay my fingers wide, bringing my thumbs together just hinting at a tease between his cheeks.

The first time I touched Cam like that, I was so tentative, daring to slide my fingers beneath his open jeans. Fucking terrified of doing the wrong thing. But he'd shuddered in my arms and breathlessly came on my stomach.

It was the hottest moment of my life.

"More control now," he rasps against my ear, telling me he's with me. Even when *with me* means four years ago.

"Yeah?"

Reaching behind him, he nods, blindly letting us in and then pressing me into the wall beside the door. "Yeah."

Our eyes meet, and I slide my hand over his fly, squeezing the steely length of him. "Whatever control you've found? I'm going to break it."

And then I spin him around so it's his back to the wall... and drop to my knees.

Cam

TREVOR HAS NO IDEA. My control broke the second I found him back in town.

That conversation at dinner, having him actually tell me how his life isn't in a place that leaves him available for a relationship just brought reality back into focus. It reminded me that self-preservation is a thing. That we have the chance to be smart. All well and good until I touched him again and realized that protecting my heart stopped mattering.

For years I regretted not taking the chance we had.

And while he isn't offering me the same thing now that he was then, I'll take it anyway.

I'll take what we can have, while we have it, and deal with the aftermath when it comes.

For now though?

He reverses our positions, and when I'm the one

with the wall holding me up— and it has to be because my knees are fucking jelly —this man who's been the longest-starring member of my fantasies drops to his knees and starts on my belt.

"Oh Jesus... you don't ha—"

"Want to." He pushes my fly open and frees my hard-on with a sure, confident grip. Thumb brushing over the leaking tip, his eyes haze. "*Need* to."

I nod, pretty sure I've stopped breathing, but I'm too transfixed by the hot, wet suction and nut-blowing visual of Trevor taking me into his mouth to care.

He grips my thighs, those big hands rubbing up and down as he pulls me in, takes more, and then draws back until my dick bobs free of his lips.

Ocean blue eyes meet mine.

"Lose the shirt, Captain." His always deep voice has turned gravelly rough. Sexy beyond belief. "Want to see you while I suck you off."

Holy shit.

My hands shakily work the buttons as he watches, jerking me with slow, firm strokes.

I shrug out of one arm and groan as Trevor rubs over his fly. Then, time sort of stutters. My shirt is on the floor and I'm watching his mouth drag over me again and again, each time giving me the wet rub of his tongue and then the deep pulling suction that has the nerves tingling along my spine.

He wasn't lying about wanting to look at me, either. His hot eyes are practically burning over my chest and shoulders. We push into fast-forward, his motions coming quick, my lungs working at triple time. I catch a glimpse of him jacking himself, the purple head of his cock pumping through his fist as he takes me into the snug hold of his throat and–

"Fuck!"

Lightning shoots through my body, wracking me with pleasure so intense it feels like it's burned through to my soul. Gasping, I watch as Trevor swallows me down, his eyes clamped shut as his own release strikes.

I see it then. Clear as day.

I'm signing up for pain. This is a heartbreak guaranteed to happen. But it doesn't stop me from urging Trevor to his feet and kissing him again. Licking into his mouth to taste us together. Threading my fingers through his hair to hold him close.

We need to clean up. We need to talk. But as we stand here sharing breath, the only thing I can manage is to ask for the one thing I can't live without.

"Stay."

DORSEY'S DOESN'T OPEN until noon on Sundays, and I've never in my life been so grateful to be able to sleep in.

Trevor is a snuggler. He's a big, muscle-bound beast of a man who crushes it on the ice and makes this almost purring sound when he pulls me into him while he's sleeping.

Yes. I watched him sleep.

I'm telling myself it wasn't the creepy kind of watching someone sleep, but the amazed and slightly disbelieving kind.

Seriously, how is this beautiful creature in my bed?

And we're back to the not-creepy sleep-watching, because the sight of his blond bedhead and bare chest against my navy plaid sheets is like a fucking revelation. And those eyelashes—

Oops. Are opening.

"You watching me?" he rasps, reaching for me and pulling me in again with another contented sound that's almost as good as the one from the middle of the night.

"Yep. Total creeper." Guess even if I'm not ready to be straight with myself, I am with him.

He chuckles gruffly, pressing the stubble of his hard-cut jaw against my shoulder and then opening his mouth to bite it.

Fuuck, I like that.

Almost as much as the fact that he didn't startle out of bed, going from zero to sixty excuses for why he needs to leave in two seconds flat.

"You want coffee?" I ask, teasing his foot with mine. "Made some not too long ago."

He hums appreciatively and drags himself up to sit, elbows resting on the spread of his knees, hands scrubbing over the back of his head. "Give me a minute and I'll be in."

"Take your time. There's a new toothbrush on the side of the sink."

I've got the coffee poured and hand him a mug when he meets me in the kitchen wearing a pair of black boxer briefs and the same smile I've been admiring since he moved to town in the eighth grade.

My kitchen isn't huge, but its U-shaped layout is perfect for him to lean into one corner and me in the other, our feet just touching.

This is the kind of morning I could get used to all too easily.

Which means it's time for a reality check.

I take a swallow of coffee and hold the mug in my hands, watching as Trevor does the same. Time to man up. "Last night was incredible."

He visibly tenses, meeting me with wary eyes. "More than that, even."

"But in the light of day, I've got to ask if it's something you want more of. Because if you ask me, the answer is yes. But—"

"Yes." There's nothing halfway about it. He sets his coffee on the stretch of counter between us and steps closer. "If you do, I do. No question."

I can't help smiling and then smiling bigger when his grin matches mine. Christ, it feels good to be with this man. For however long I get to keep him.

"Good. You know I do. But"— I set my coffee mug

next to his, trying not to get caught up in how nice they look together — "even with some of the complications stripped away, there are some we can't ignore."

He nods. "Like what does this look like for the next few weeks?"

I take an unsteady breath because the more this clarifies in my mind, the less I like it. But I think I need it. "I don't want to ask you to be my secret or to feel like we're hiding. But at the same time, I know how easily I could get carried away with you. And if this isn't going to last, I guess... I just don't want everyone who's been waiting for me to find a nice man and settle down thinking it's happened."

Those big blue eyes hold steady. He's taking this seriously and, damn, I appreciate it. "So what do you want them to think? That we're just friends?"

I give him a hard shake of my head but then soften, realizing I don't know. What might be right for me might not be right for him. "If that's what you want, then okay. Maybe it's the simplest solution we've got."

He reaches for my hand. "Or?"

"Or we don't hide what we're doing. But in public, and only in public, we tone down *this* part." I nod to where he's now holding my hand in both of his. "I don't care if they think we're hooking up. If it looks like we're having some kind of summer fling."

One heavy blond brow lifts, the corner of his mouth pushing into a sexy slant that makes my heart skip and my body heat. "So, I can give you all the fuck-me eyes I want?"

I nod, reacting to the eyes he's giving me now. "If that's what you want. Yeah."

He looks me over then. Slowly. Nostrils flaring as he sees me getting hard beneath his stare.

Voice low, he goes on, "Drag you out of parties before they're over..."

Is this real? "Before they've even started."

"Buy lube in bulk..."

I cough out a laugh, pushing my dick down. Not that it does much good when he closes the distance between us, brushing my hand aside to replace it with his.

Oh God.

"N-Not sure Dean's Pharmacy carries it in bulk," I croak, emotion and need churning within me, the squeeze of his hand driving me to the edge.

He hums, leaning closer so I can feel the barest hint of his stubble scrape against mine. His breath, warm against my neck. "I'll order online."

And that's it. I break. Grabbing him by the back of the head, I pull him to me for a hard kiss with one hand while the other slides into his boxers to stroke him.

He grunts against my mouth, opening to the thrust of my tongue as he pushes into my hold. Hips flexing, he gives me another mind-wrecking squeeze before releasing, but only to push the fabric out of the way and grip me in his fist.

I've fantasized about this. For years. Remembering the taste of his kiss, the feel of his hand on me, tentative at first and then bolder. Pretending my touch was his. But no fantasy compares to this.

Mouths fused, hearts slamming, we kiss harder, deeper. Our tongues rolling over and against each other. Sliding and stroking as our hands do the same.

I shudder against him, aching within his hold while pumping his steely length in mine.

Fuck, he's perfect. Thick and hot with enough precum leaking from his slit to run down my thumb.

He's perfect, growling and gasping as he crowds me into the corner and, again, brushes my hand aside. This time so he can line us up and take both our cocks in his massive hand. I look down, breath locked in the vise of my chest. And seeing our bulbous heads together like that, side by side, his a shade darker, mine a bit wider, both glistening with every firm jerk of his fist—

Perfect.

It's too good. Too hot. Too hard and fast and so fucking right. And when I see another swell of pearly liquid push from his slit and run over mine...

"Need to make you come," he grits out, firming his hold even more.

Pressure and relief surge through me as Trev takes my mouth in another claiming kiss.

Moaning around the hard thrust of his tongue, I give in, coming over his fingers in hot spurts that slick up his hold. Jesus, the sounds he makes when it happens... it's like he's the one who finished instead of me.

His mouth tears from mine, and he looks down at his hand covered in my release before meeting my eyes again.

"Cam," he gasps, following me over with a breathless, shuddering release that's more beautiful than anything I've ever seen before.

Eyes still locked with mine, he shakes his head. "That was... *fuck*. Gonna have to do that again." He takes another, slower breath and smiles at me.

That smile is like the sun.

And God, I want him. I want everything.

Just so long as it doesn't look like we're falling in love. Because when he's gone, it's going to be painful enough for me to deal with the fact that I already have without the whole town knowing it too.

8

Trevor

I was joking about the lube. Mostly.

We both had some on hand and, even though we haven't actually gone *there*, when we used it up this morning... I realized I really was going to have to make an emergency run to the pharmacy for more.

Not going to lie though, there is a thirty-two-ounce pump bottle sitting in my Prime cart, and over the past week I've come within a heartbeat of clicking the purchase button more than once. The only thing that's keeping me from doing it is that I don't want to be a pushy motherfucker. I don't want Cam thinking I need us to take that last step.

Because maybe it's the line we don't cross for a reason.

I mean, yeah, there's something about Cam that begs me to go all in. Even knowing we can't be anything more than temporary, every time I see this guy, my heart feels like it's trying to tear down my ribs to get to him.

Holding back is a challenge I wasn't expecting, but this one emotional discretion matters to him. So even though we've been *out* in town together— I pulled him in for a kiss when I met him at the bar the other night and, not surprisingly, the whole town knew by the next day —I have managed to fight the impulse to bring Cam a coffee every single morning and park myself on the couch in front of the bass-fishing show with all the geezers just so I can be close to him throughout the day. Watch as he stocks shelves and helps customers in his hot-as-hell Outfitters T-shirt. Ask him to show me how to hold my rod when he goes on break.

Ugh.

I've been good. All week. Which is why the second his truck pulled to a stop in front of my place last night? Yeah, the poor guy didn't even have a chance to turn the engine off before I had his door open and was hauling him out.

Demanding a reward for my restraint— and a *reward* is exactly what having him breathless above me, fingers knotted in my hair as his come shoots down my throat, is.

So hot.

Not what I need to be thinking about standing in line behind my old lunch lady at Dean's.

"Gulls, thought that was you."

I turn, finding Neil beside me, eying the *not-fooling-anyone* bottle of Scope, bag of jerky, and generously sized but no thirty-two-ounce container of lube in my basket.

Not embarrassed. We're all adults here.

"Hey, Watson. Good to see you again." Neil was at the bar the other night when we met up with a bunch of the water polo players from Cam's team. Not that I had much of a chance to catch up with him, the way he and Judy were huddled together in a corner like they were the only ones left on the planet.

It was cute to see, especially after the way the guy used to moon after her in high school.

Now, there's something distinctly not cute about the look he's leveling me with. In fact, there's something downright menacing about it. Which is saying a lot, considering Neil has a Cosmo magazine and a box of tampons tucked under his arm.

"Everything okay?"

"Sure. Sure, it is." He smiles. Flatly. "You know Cam's my best friend. *Right?*"

My brows lift. *Well, damn.*

~

"I SWEAR TO GOD, Cam, he was giving me the talk," I say, handing him a beer and then dropping onto the opposite side of the couch and propping my feet beside his on the table. "Like *you-break-his-heart-I-break-your-face* style."

Cam's shaking his head, lips parted in one of those stunted laughs. "No."

"Yes." We clink our longnecks. "Hundred percent, yes. He *flexed* at me."

Damn, that laugh. This guy was always so reserved in high school. But now, he's always laughing, and I freaking love it.

"Now I know you're lying to me."

"I'm not." My head drops back against the cushions, and I sigh. "And it was *awesome*."

He shifts so he's got one gorgeous, musclebound arm stretched across the top of the couch and he's facing me. "I talked to him. Told him not to get carried away about you and me being together. That we're just having some fun."

"Ehh, he's your ride or die. Neil's probably excited for a chance to be the one looking out for you for a change, right?" I thread our fingers together. "Unless you think he's jealous and this decades-long business with Judy is all part of some long game to get with you... in which case, my *flex* is totes bigger than his *flex*."

I demonstrate, popping some muscles for show

and earning a hard eye roll and more of the smile I can't get enough of.

"Baby, put those things away." And then after another sip of beer, he leans back, relaxed. "So, tell me about the call with your agent today. She got any good news for you?"

Ahh, that. "Not really. Mostly rumors, conversations. Nothing solid enough to actually hold on to, you know?"

But damned if it isn't nice to be able to share it with him.

Cam nods. "What's she hearing?"

"That Boomer's looking good. He's been working with trainers, getting on the ice every chance he's got."

"Boomer? That's the player you were filling in for?"

"Yeah. Ben Boerboom."

"You ever meet him?" he asks, wincing like it would be weird, but I laugh him off.

"After they cleared him to start working out again. Nice guy, funny. But not what I was expecting."

Cam lifts a brow, always more curious about the person than the player.

"It's like Boomer's got the rep. About everything. He's some epic goof. He's a hothead. He's the biggest *player* on the team. All these larger-than-life labels, but I didn't really see it. Yeah, he's kind of over-the-top, but when it comes to his game the guy is serious as a heart attack. And as far as women? He seemed more concerned about what was happening with his buddy and little sister than making nice with the bunnies hanging around outside the arena."

Cam chuckles. "You like him."

"I like *all* of them." I tilt my beer back, let the cool liquid roll over my tongue, and then take a slow breath. "It's such a weird spot to be in. My moving up means someone else moving on. Moving over."

"Moving out of your way."

Yeah. That.

"I want to play. *Fuck*, I want it so bad. Even more so now that I've had the chance to get out there with the team. And it was *good*." I meet Cam's eyes, letting him see everything in mine. "If I had the chance, it would only get better. I know it would."

"You were amazing out there. Can't believe what you can do, Trev. And whoever makes the decisions on this stuff saw it too. They're going to want you back."

I rub at the spot in my chest that warms from his praise, the conviction in his voice even though hockey isn't something he's ever really followed and doesn't know much about. It means something that he believes in me.

"I've been fighting to beat out other players, friends, guys who want it every bit as bad as me, for as far back as I can remember. And yeah, you always feel for the guys who didn't make it. But it's okay, because you know going in... you're all fighting for something that doesn't belong to anyone yet. But this?"

"Hey." He leans forward, giving my arm a squeeze

and then brushing the skin with his thumb. "You can't feel bad about wanting a spot. I know you've got a big heart, but so far as I understand it, hockey is like every other competitive sport out there. You get to keep your wins and trophies. Your stats. That stuff is yours.

"But your spot in the lineup? Your time on the ice? That you have to keep fighting for, every single game, meet, match, whatever. And every athlete at your level knows it. Right? It's not personal. It's not like you're starting a smear campaign or spreading misinformation. You're playing your hardest, because that's your job. And if they ask you back, it's because they believe you're going to make the team stronger than it would be without you."

I nod, afraid to open my mouth. Because the words are there, ready to jump the boards to get out. Christ, I want to say it.

I love you.

I feel it like a physical thing. But breaking all our rules is no way to repay this man for saying exactly what I need to hear.

Cam

IT's TOO easy imagining this man in my life beyond the two weeks we have left together. Two weeks. Every time I think about that ticking clock and what my life is going to look like after Trevor's gone, my chest gets that unnatural, too-tight feeling of holding my breath at the bottom of the pool.

I don't like it, but I just keep diving back in regardless. Because this, the way things have been between us since he got back here, is *everything*.

We've been together every night. Sometimes at his place. Sometimes at mine. Always when we close our eyes and still when we pry them open in the morning.

It's so good, but it's just a fling.

I try to convince myself that's the magic of it— the whole no-expectations-beyond-the-end-of-the-month thing. That we're living outside of reality, and *that's* why it's so easy, so effortless.

Maybe I'd be able to believe my own bull if it wasn't for one little thing... we've been here before.

Back in high school, Trevor and I ran in different circles. He played hockey and I swam. Both winter sports, which meant that even in a community as small as Wildren, there was a divide. It wasn't hostile, but people had to choose how they spent their Friday nights. And those choices carried over into lunches and the time between the bells during the school days too.

So while we were *friendly*... we weren't really *friends*.

But somehow, any time we ended up in the same

space— paired up for badminton in gym class, dissecting a cow eye in biology, or waiting in the hall to be called in for the vision test— something just clicked.

We laughed at the same jokes and got exactly what the other was saying, whether it was debating the merits of fries over tater tots or falling into that one shockingly intimate conversation about me losing my mom and him losing his dad in grade school.

We clicked so well, it scared me. And at a time when I was still working so hard to keep my secret, there was this boy who made me feel like anyone walking by could see what I was thinking about him.

Worse, that *he* would.

There were times I avoided him for that alone. And then times when I got reckless and leaned into that easy connection just for a minute, just praying that no one would notice. That's what I was doing the night of Finch's party.

Following him out to the lake after that dare– just to make sure he was good –was *reckless*, but I couldn't resist. Just like I can't resist now.

The risk isn't the same. It's higher. Because every night we spend together with him telling me about the players he skates with and me sharing stories from my water polo season, every time he decides to try to teach me to cook something and then has to kick me out of the kitchen to save it... every time we fall into bed, tearing at each other's clothes with a desperation beyond my imagination makes me see how perfect this could be... if only everything about our lives was different.

I know the hurt is coming. I know saying goodbye again is going to wreck me. But after all the years of living in fear, maybe my reserves of self-preservation are exhausted. Or maybe being able to go all in with this man and having this month without holding back is worth whatever heartbreak comes after.

Trevor

FOR A GUY ON BREAK, I'm managing to keep damn busy... which is critical to ignoring the fact that I'm about one week from ripping my heart out and leaving it here in Wildren.

Don't think about it.

So in addition to keeping up with my conditioning, catching up with old friends, and the odd jobs I'm knocking out at Finch's place... I got permission to use the high school gym to work out and the rink to offer a few free hockey clinics in the afternoons. Coach tells me there's some real talent on the team this year, and it's cool to be able to share my knowledge and experience with kids who have the same love of the sport as me.

But what makes my damn decade is when Cam

shows up with his cousin's tiny five-year-old to the open skate for the mini-mites. She's pink from head to toe, outfit, cheeks, even the strawberry-blond curls... and already you can see this little firecracker likes to win. She skates like a demon and makes no bones about picking the puck up off her kindergarten friend's sticks. It's hilarious and a little scary, but not nearly so much as watching my semi-secret boyfriend... who I've never seen skate for a reason... fall on his taut, perfect ass.

"*What* were you doing today?" I laugh, walking into Cam's place a few hours later and finding him tossing back a couple ibuprofen.

"Probably fucking up my water polo match tomorrow night, but mostly looking for an excuse to see you."

Damn, *this guy*.

"I both love and hate that answer." I take the bottle from him and put it back in the cabinet above the toaster.

"You're awesome with those kids," he says, sidling up to me and hooking a finger through my belt loop. "Betsy told her mom she was going to grow up and play on your hockey team. Which is bullshit, by the way, since last week she was planning to play water polo with me."

Slipping my arms around his waist, I kiss the underside of his jaw. "Stings, huh?"

And that answering laugh rumbling against my chest is something else. It's the kind of addicting sound someone could get hooked on, even if he knows he shouldn't.

"You hurt for real?" I ask, hating that he might be.

He shakes his head and gives me a wink. "Nah. I'm tough." And when he sees my concern is real, he adds, "Seriously, it's nothing loosening up with a swim won't take care of."

"Practice tonight?" I didn't think he had one. And yeah, I've gotten familiar with his calendar.

"Tomorrow. But I'm thinking about hitting the lake before dinner. You mind?"

"Not even a little. In fact, I've got ingredients for chicken piccata in the fridge. Maybe I'll head back and start it. Or"— I let my hands do a little shameless wandering over his ass, pressing into him in a tease I'll absolutely be regretting until I get him naked again— "maybe I'll meet you on our dock. Hang out a while, and we can save dinner for later?"

That groan is everything and, no surprise, we end up making out with my back to his fridge and him sucking on my tongue while we rock into each other. It's too good, but I don't want him swimming in the dark so I pull away, giving his hard-on a parting caress.

"See you in a few." I start for the door.

"Hold up," he calls after me. "I got a couple bottles that'll go great with your dinner."

I have no idea what pairs with piccata, but I nod and wait. My phone pings with a text from Static. Cam's still rustling around in the kitchen so I skim the team gossip, coughing out a laugh when I read what just happened to Boomer. Holy shit.

"Here, take this over for me?" Cam says, pulling my attention back to the now as he hands me a loaded reusable grocery bag.

"No problem." This time the kiss is just a sweet peck that leaves me humming as I back toward the truck. "Swim fast, Captain."

He hooks his hands on the frame above the door and leans out with a cocky grin. "State champ."

So. Hot.

I drive home wearing a stupid grin I feel through every cell in my body. I'll get the chicken out, then grab my trunks and a couple towels. We could eat on the back terrace.

Talk.

Talk about whether this really needs to end when I leave. If maybe there's a way we can—

I frown as I pull into my drive and catch a glimpse of another car through the trees. Being this far outside of town, it's not a place people drop by unannounced. So who?

Realtors? Squatters? Burglars?

But then I clear the trees and—

No.

Hell, no.

I pull to a stop, dread pooling in my gut. I know exactly who this asshole unfolding from the front step is.

Leo. My ex.

9

_____

Cam

I f there were a touch pad sensor on the floating swim dock in front of Trevor's, I'm pretty confident today would be my personal best time yet. And even without the timer, the fact that I beat him says I was blazing.

Either that, or maybe he liked the look of the bottle I sent and started without me? Ever the optimist — at least since Trevor pulled back into town three and a half weeks ago —I swim to shore and then start up to the cabin.

Halfway there, I hear it— *"I love you, T."* —and I trip over my next step.

Suddenly, it feels like I swallowed a gallon of lake water. Like it's in my lungs, choking me. In my legs, weighing me down. In my gut, making me sick.

I climb faster.

"Leo... you love me?"

The sound of Trevor's stunned laugh filters around the house, muted to the point that I can't read the emotion in it. Joy or disgust, I have no idea. All I know is that I need to be there. I need to see this mother-fucker who broke my boyfriend's heart... and I need to see what Trevor looks like when he looks at him.

Because suddenly the only thing I can think about is Neil and Judy and Harvey. And I'm realizing that if Trevor goes back to this jerk, I'm going to usurp Neil as Captain of the simp squad and be everything I begged my buddy to stop being. The friend. The rebound. Anything I can get.

I hear the door from the truck slam and gravel crushing underfoot as Trevor's voice carries to me loud and clear. "I don't think you know what that word means."

Rounding the side of the house, I play like I'm not about to die inside. Like I don't have a single thing to worry about.

Raising a hand, I push my mouth into a slanted smile, barely sparing a glance at the built asshole standing in front of my boyfriend with a look of confusion and heartbreak in his eyes.

"Hey, babe. That was some workout." I toss my goggles by the front stoop, striding into Trevor's space, dripping wet and acting like the possessive dickhead I've become in the last two minutes.

I lean down and kiss him on the mouth. Not jamming my tongue down his throat, but for a lingering beat... *like he's fucking mine.*

It ought to be enough. But in for a penny, in for a pound. So I add, "Almost as good as the one you gave me last night."

He coughs, blue eyes going wide as they search mine like they're wondering who the hell took over my body.

From behind me, I hear the ex mutter a curse. And then, "Jesus Christ, you're... the goddamn *swimmer*?"

Huh?

Surprise more than anything turns me around. The prick is staring at me, sizing me up. Whatever. Crossing my arms, I step in beside Trevor... who's also still watching me, the slightest hitch at the corner of his mouth.

Gonna take that as a good sign. I turn back to the ex. "Guess so. Cam Dorsey."

"Yeah. Leo." He shifts uncomfortably, but then gives it up. "Leo Rossi. I'm uhh... Trevor's roommate. We play for the same team."

And now I get why even when Trevor was telling me about this relationship, he was so careful with the details. Nothing to indicate who this man was. No dots to connect.

This fucker has no idea the respect Trevor has given his privacy.

"Do you play for the Slayers too?"

He blinks, and a flash of jealousy drifts over his face before he wipes it away. "No, I'm down in Springfield with the Orators. Hey, man, you want to give us a minute here?"

That would be a hard no. I really don't. But I turn to Trevor, and the corner of his mouth is hitched even higher. "Is that what you want?"

For him, I would. But Trevor shakes his head and threads our fingers together. "Nope. You belong here. If Leo's got something to say, he can say it in front of you. Or he can go. Either way, it isn't going to change anything."

I swallow past a surge of emotion, nodding with a smile I'll give him the words to match when we're alone.

Leo ducks his head. "Come on, T. You know it's not over. Not because of this guy."

"It is over."

I raise a brow, but Leo just grinds his molars together and blows out a breath. "Fine. You want to get yours? Okay. I deserve it after how I hurt you. You've got another week. Screw everyone in the state if you like. Get it out of your system, and I'll see you at training camp." He bites his lip and flexes his chest. "Just like last year."

I feel Trevor's hand tense in mine, and my blood starts to boil. In twenty-two years I've never been in a fight. Never even thought about taking a swing at someone, but those careless, condescending words have me finally understanding the urge to do violence.

"Wow, quite the offer." Trevor shakes his head in disgust. "But there's nothing to figure out, Leo. It's over. If you've worked your shit out, I'm happy for you. If you haven't… not my problem. But yeah, I'll see you at camp. I'll be the 'out' hockey player fighting for a spot on the Slayers' roster. And you'll be just another player on the ice."

Leo pales, hands coming up. "Hold on. *Out?* You can't do that to me, man. We were roommates. We *lived together*. What will people think?"

Trevor shrugs. "They'll think you had a roommate who dates men. And I guess it's up to you if you want to be someone who didn't care or someone who did. Or even someone who dated me but made mistakes, learned from them, and is in a better place now. Whatever you do, Leo, it's up to you and it's *on* you. And… honestly, I wish you the best. But I'm ready to cook some chicken and spend the night with the guy I love."

I've been listening, offering my quiet support to this point, but now—

Did he just say—

I turn to him, pulling his hand close to my pounding heart. He loves me?

Trevor ducks to kiss my knuckles as Leo rounds his SUV in a huff and slams the door. Neither of us look as he drives away. Because what matters is this. Now.

"Love, huh?" I ask in a voice choked with emotion.

"From that first night, Cam. All those years ago. I loved you then, and I love you now. And even though I understand the kind of life I have to offer you can never compete with the life you have here, I just... I want you to know that if it could... I'd love you forever."

My heart cracks open right then and there. Pulling Trevor into my arms, I kiss him hard and deep and with everything I have. I kiss him like I love him because the truth of it is that simple. I do. And when I break away, it's just enough to whisper against his lips, "I never stopped. I love you too."

Trevor

HE LOVES ME. I don't know if my heart can take what those words are doing to it.

Kissing, we stumble toward the house. Our hands are everywhere, his suit is soaking my shorts, and all I can think is...

Keep him.

I need to find a way. I'll do anything. But first, I need to show him how much I worship him.

We make it inside, and Cam whips my shirt over my head, growling as he pushes me toward the bedroom, his mouth on my neck, my shoulders, my chest.

"Love you," I pant, when I feel the bite of his teeth followed by the pull of deep suction at my shoulder.

"Love you," he rasps, maneuvering me into my room. "So fucking much."

My legs meet the bed, but before I tumble back, I shift my weight, pulling him around so it's his body falling beneath mine. I lick through his navel and nibble the side of that sexy vee as I pry my fingers into the insanely snug jammers and peel them off.

"Christ, you're gorgeous." I can barely manage the words through everything I'm feeling. The love, the purpose, the need... and the knowledge that even with my soul so full of all of those things, it still might not be enough to keep him. If I gave up hockey, would he even want me to start a life with him here?

It's a question I need to think through, figure out how to finesse and present in a way that doesn't pressure or overwhelm him.

It's a question that's going to have to wait.

Cam jackknifes up to sit, his hands holding the sides of my head as he kisses me. Then he pulls back to meet my eyes. "I want you. I need you inside me."

I freeze, my body and mind on the brink of short-circuiting at the visuals bombarding me. We've used our mouths and our hands. Our fingers. But we've stopped just short of actual penetrative sex, neither one of us bringing it up as if we both knew it would take us to a connection too deep for the limits we were trying to preserve.

But now? "Are you saying—"

"I want us to be together."

I cover his mouth with mine, pulling our bodies as close as we can get with me still half dressed.

"Where's the bag?" he rasps against my lips.

I pull back. "The bag with the *wine*?"

He nods, wrapping his hand around his cock and giving it a torturously slow tug. Damn, that's hot.

So hot that it takes me a second to realize what he's asking for. Wine. Because he wants something to help him relax a little?

I nod, taking a step back from the bed, eyes still riveted to where his fingers have moved over his balls and... lower.

"Be right back."

I run for the front of the house, leaping off the stoop to grab the bag I left on the drive next to the truck. Then I'm tearing back in, sliding into the bedroom before I realize— "Shit! Glasses and an opener. One second."

"Wait!" Cam's sitting up, that hand that was having all the fun a second ago, now held up in a plea for me to stop. And he's laughing.

Which I *love* to see but don't understand. "What?"

He points to the bag I'm clutching in my arms like a baby. "Just, um... you want to take a look in there?"

No. I want to devour him with my mouth, tease

him open with my fingers and tongue. I want to make him come so hard he forgets every man he's ever been with before me.

But for him, I set the bag on the bed and realize there's more than just a bottle of wine inside. Curious, I peek in and choke on a laugh.

10

Trevor

The wine comes out first. I set it on the floor. Close enough in case he actually wants some. But I'm getting the sense maybe it's the *other* bottle he's after.

Like the gigantic, how-did-I-miss-this, sixty-four-ounce pump bottle of lube.

I lift my brow. "Think it'll be enough?"

Cam's got the sexiest, most adorable pink tint burning over his cheeks. "For tonight? Probably."

I nod, extracting the next item. A far more conservative box of thirty condoms.

"I love you." I can't say it enough, don't know if I'll ever be able to.

"Then show me." Cocking one knee, he teases me with a view that takes my breath away.

My shorts and underwear hit the floor point two seconds later, and then I'm kissing and biting my way up his long, sexy leg, rubbing my face against his inner thigh and nuzzling beneath his sac.

He pulls me higher, begging for my kiss and then begging for more. I fill my palm and his with the slippery liquid and rub it over his shaft and balls, getting impossibly harder when I add more and generously rub it over his needy hole before sliding a finger in.

I pump slowly, in and out. Warming him up with one finger before adding another.

We kiss and tease, sliding together as I work him open. I take my time, watching carefully. Neither of us are virgins, but this will be *our* first time, and I want to make it good for him. I want him to feel how much I love him. To know that he is my world.

I press deep, stroking over his prostate and reveling in the way he starts to shake and gasp.

"Need... you to... oh God, baby... Need you to fuck me."

Shifting onto my knees between his legs, I roll on a condom and cover it with more lube before lining the tip up with where he's waiting for me. Then slowly, carefully, I push inside.

"Relax for me, Captain," I whisper, shifting my weight forward to lean over him as I give him more, push deeper. As he lets me make his precious, perfect body mine the way my whole damn heart is his.

Our eyes meet, and a ghost of a smile flickers over his parted lips.

And it's perfect.

It's love.

It's worth so much more than the career I thought was my whole life. More than the place where I live. More than all the million things that occupied my life before I found him again.

"Never letting you go," I grunt, something savage and primal taking over as I piston inside him, angling my hips to make sure I'm hitting that sweet spot with every thrust. "Never going to leave."

He's shaking beneath me, gasping my name as our sweat-slicked bodies move together, as each thrust comes harder.

"More," he begs.

I give him more, his pleasure fueling mine.

"Harder... *God, like that.*"

I'll give him anything, everything.

"Trevor!" He throbs around me, his release painting my stomach and his with ropes of come.

And that's it. I'm done. Lightning races up my spine and I shout, coming inside him like I'm coming home.

Cam

I CAN HEAR the waves rolling in against the shore as the sky beyond Trevor's bedroom windows dims. We're lying together beneath the sheet, his big, muscly arm over my shoulder as my head rests against his chest. It's perfect.

After we cleaned up, we climbed back into bed and maybe even dozed a while. But mostly, I think we just wanted to *be*.

Here.

Quiet.

Together.

But it's time.

Tracing the lines of his chest with my fingers, I peer up at him. "Think now that the heat of the moment has cooled a little, you want to talk?"

His chest stops moving. "That what it was? The heat of the moment?"

I shake my head, shifting so I'm more on top of him than not. "It *was* hot. And yeah, we were caught up some. But no, not entirely."

Trevor brushes my hair from my eyes. "I love you."

Direct and to the point. This is the man from four years ago. The one who knew what he wanted from the start and, afraid or not, went after it.

"I love you too. So we both meant what we said about that."

He swallows, those beautiful eyes searching mine. "I meant what I said about everything. I can't leave you again. I won't."

I blink. He's not saying what I think he's saying.

"Hockey?" I choke out through a tightening throat.

But he's already shaking his head. "I choose you."

My heart goes into free fall, and this time I can't even form words. But he's there, rubbing his hand over my shoulder and arm, touching me like he needs the contact as much as I do.

"Cam, if— if that's too fast or you don't feel comfortable yet—"

"No." Pushing up on my arms, I brace above him to take a kiss and breathe him in. "Not too fast."

It's four years past the time I should have grabbed him with both arms and never let go. "It's just there are more options here than you giving up your career. The sport you love. *Your dream.* Because, yeah, I know that's what this is. I remember lying out in that field beneath the stars all those years ago and you telling me you'd been dreaming of playing hockey since you were old enough to put on skates."

"Yeah, and you told me the only thing you'd ever wanted was to run your dad's store with him. It's the reason we broke up. This town, this life is *your* dream and it's no less important than mine. Besides, dreams change. Mine is being with you."

And mine is spending the rest of my life working to be worthy of the kind of love this man is giving me.

"Trevor, listen—"

But he isn't ready. "Why would you come with me? I can't offer you stability. Hell, after training camp, I have no idea which city I'll even be living in. If it's like the end of last season, it could be both. It could be like that for a long time. And then there's the travel. You'd be left alone—"

"Trev, that stuff— hell, I don't know what that will be like, but we can figure it out as we go. That stuff isn't stability to me. *You are.* Having someone I love who loves me back. Someone who wants our life, whatever it looks like and wherever it takes us, to be... together."

His face twists like he's in pain. "I don't want to wreck your life."

"Then don't make me watch you sacrifice who you are and everything you've worked for because you think it's what I need."

"But you love it here. Your whole life is here."

Taking his hand in mine, I hold it to my heart. "I do love it here. And I expect we'll spend a lot of vacations here. We can have both. I'll find a team to swim on or play water polo with during your season. I'll watch your games and meet your friends. I'll— *we'll* build a life that we can love together."

I wait for his argument, ready to talk it through all night or however long it takes for him to see, to believe. But then the most magical, amazing fucking thing happens. A tentative smile breaks across his lips.

My heart starts to hammer, and I kiss him hard and quick, pulling back to see that smile stretch as he begins to nod with me. "So we're doing this? Really?"

"Yeah, Trevor." I laugh and kiss him again. "We're really doing it."

And then he's laughing too, his eyes tearing up. "I don't know what to say."

"Why don't you tell me you love me again, because I don't think I'll ever get tired of hearing it."

"I love you. I'm so damn in love with you, I can barely see straight. And I'm totally bringing you coffee tomorrow and watching you ring up sales in that hot freaking shirt all day."

Him and that shirt. "The guys will be thrilled."

And they are.

~

Thank you for reading DIRTY-DARE!
I've had the most fun with these guys, and it means the world to me that you chose to spend some time with them.

Boomer's up next with DIRTY FLIRT.
Or if you're new to Slayers Hockey, go back to the beginning with DIRTY SECRET.

Want to stay in touch?
Sign up for my Newsletter
And
Join my Facebook Reader Group

And for a list of all my books, turn to the next page or hop on over to my website at miralynkelly.com

THE WEDDING DATE BOOKS

MAY THE BEST MAN WIN (Jase & Emily)

THE WEDDING DATE BARGAIN (Max & Sara)

JUST THIS ONCE (Sean & Molly)

DECOY DATE (Brody & Gwen)

COMING AROUND AGAIN (Re-releases from my early Mira Lyn Kelly & Moira McTark days)

(Connected, 1st Person POV)

Just Friends (Matt & Nikki)

All In (Lanie & Jason)

(Unconnected, 3rd Person POV)

Front Page Affair (Nate & Payton)

The S Before Ex (Ryan & Claire)

Waking Up Married (Connor & Megan)

Once is Never Enough (Garrett & Nichole)

ACKNOWLEDGMENTS

Fun fact: There's more to creating a book than writing the words alone. A lot more!

The magic that goes into each story that finds its way onto your eReader or shelf extends from that first willing ear past the last set of eyes checking for typos. And I am beyond grateful for every single one of the people continually proving that writing is a team sport.

So huge thanks to Lexi Ryan, Jennifer Haymore, Autumn Gantz at Wordsmith Publicity, Zoe York, Kara Hildebrand, Becca Syne, Skye Warren, Najla Qamber Designs, Tara Carberry at Dreamscape Media, and my incredible agent Nicole Resciniti.

To all my friends from Write All The Words, everyone from Hockey Ever After and the Book Bunnies, my Promo team and Eagle Eyes, and the reviewers and bloggers who help me spread the word about my books. To my family who puts up with my crazy hours and pig pen office and my friends who are the best break from deadline crazy.

And especially to you! Thank you for reading.

((HUGS)) Mira

ABOUT THE AUTHOR

Hard core romantic, stress baker, and housekeeper non-extraordinaire, Mira Lyn Kelly is the USA TODAY bestselling author of more than two dozen sizzly love stories with over a million readers worldwide. Growing up in the Chicago area, she earned her degree in Fine Arts from Loyola University and met the love of her life while studying abroad in Rome, Italy... only to discover he'd been living right around the corner from her back home. Having spent her twenties working and playing in the Windy City, she's now settled with her family in Minnesota.

www.miralynkelly.com

Looking to stay in touch and keep up with my new releases, sales and giveaways?? Join my newsletter at miralynkelly.com/newsletter and my Facebook reader group at MiraLynKelly's Book Bunnies. We'd love to have you!!